I0843510

THE SPARROW WILL *Fly*

DINK KEARNEY

The Sparrow Will Fly
Copyright © 2025 by Dink Kearney.

All rights reserved. No part of this book may be reproduced in any form or by any electronic or mechanical means, including information storage and retrieval systems, without permission in writing from the publisher and author, except by reviewers, who may quote brief passages in a review.

This publication contains the opinions and ideas of its author. It is intended to provide helpful and informative material on the subjects addressed in the publication. The authors and publisher specically disclaim all responsibility for any liability, loss, or risk, personal or otherwise, which is incurred as a consequence, directly or indirectly, of the use and application of any of the contents of this book.

ISBN: 978-1-966954-27-9   (Hardback)
            978-1-966954-30-9   (Paperback)
            978-1-966954-28-6   (Kindle)

I woke up feeling good that day. It was the first day of basketball practice and I couldn't wait to show my teammates and Coach Gomes that I was 6'6 feet tall and shooting 2,000 jump shots a day. Hopefully, I was tall enough and good enough to earn a basketball scholarship to play for the North Carolina State Wolfpack. The best university in the world, and I could study Zoology and become a Veterinarian.

"Isn't that right, Scooter?" I asked my brown and white Cocker Spaniel dog as I pretended to be Michael Jordan and shoot my nerf basketball into the goal. Whenever I had to go to the doctor I played basketball on my kiddy basketball goal to calm my nerves. I never liked going to the doctor. I always had to get a shot or something.

Scooter barked and jumped into my arms. Scooter agreed with me all of the time. His blood pumped Wolfpack red like mine. He was my buddy, someone to talk to when I wasn't feeling well, which had happened a lot lately. I started getting fevers and night's sweats and Mom got concerned. So I had to go back for a checkup. I felt good, though.

"Paul, let's go, we don't have all day for you and Scooter to play basketball! You have an appointment to see Dr. Moses!"

"Okay. I'll be down in one sec! Let me get my keys!" I called.

"Nope! I'm driving, "said Mom. "I want to be on time."

I petted Scooter on the head and promised him I'll bring him some doggie cookies when I returned.

As we drove down University Drive, Mom mumbled biblical scriptures and listened to the gospel station. I stared at her. Whenever she listened to gospel music and started singing, she was asking God for an answer or for strength. But I didn't know what she was asking for. Everything was good in our life, except that Dad had died in the spring. We had food, a new house, new car, and Mom had plenty of church friends and family who came over. And most of all we had fun, playing the basketball game 'Horse 'and the card game 'Spades.' But as soon as they left, the pain of not having Dad returned.

I missed Dad so much that I found myself talking to him. I would stare at the mirror and just pretend to talk to Dad about basketball, girls, and how big Scooter was getting. Of course, I talked to Dad about how I was going to be great like my favorite basketball player, LeBron James, and how many times I could dunk the ball. He gave me such much confidence. Man I missed Dad. Honestly, I had no idea how Mom dealt with Dad's death. Mom had depended on him so much. From buying groceries to paying all of the bills to her being a stay at home mom; he did everything for her. He spoiled Mom so much she barely drove a car. Poor Mom I think to myself sometimes.

"Are you okay Mom?" I asked quietly, stroking her long, Sandy Red hair.

"Oh, no worry Paul! Just thinking, thinking about how much you have grown. Wow! You're definitely a big boy now. But you're still my baby." Said Mom.

"But you only do this-" Mom held up her finger to silence me.

"All right Mom, I understand."

I don't bother Mom when she's having a spiritual moment or as I liked to say, acting like Jesus. So while Mom continued to look for spiritual guidance from the "Big Man" in the sky, I continued to dream about this upcoming basketball season: scoring 40 points against arch rival Broughton and winning the game, slam dunking on the best player in the state, Joshua Abraham, and winning the state championship. I would definitely go to NC State University then. How could the Wolfpack deny me a scholarship? And I could study and become a Veterinarian like Dad. Man was I excited.

This was going to be a great year, I thought at the time.

When we arrived at UNC Hospital and walked through the double glass doors with the dark Tar Heels logo, I became nauseated because I hated the Tar Heels basketball team because I was a diehard Wolfpack fan. And we hated the Tar Heels. For the first time, I noticed small red marks on my arm. Hmmm…better ask Dr. Moses about it. He had been my doctor since I could remember. The only thing I didn't like about him was that he was a big fan of the UNC Tar Heels, the arch rival of the NC State Wolfpack. And he would tease me whenever we would lose to UNC and he used to tell me how he would pay for my college tuition if I went to UNC, his alma mater.

I used to laugh at the silly idea.

When Mom and I entered Dr. Moses' oval- shaped office, the secretary immediately motioned for us to go straight into his office. That was unusual because we always had to wait. Mom rushed into his office, holding my hand as if I were a toddler.

Dr. Moses stood with two other doctors, holding my medical files in his arms. He put on his horn- rimmed glasses and asked us to sit down.

"Hello Mrs. Christian, and Paul," said Dr. Moses in his baritone voice. "It's good to see you all! Paul, you have grown a lot since our last visit!"

"Yes he has," said Mom, twisting her wedding band nervously, "and he's eating me out of house and home. He's excited about playing basketball, hopefully he can play?-"

Before she could finish her sentence, I said, "Of course I can play basketball. Why wouldn't I? I feel good most of the time, and I've grown like six inches over the summer. The only problems I have are fevers and night sweats…Oh and I have these red marks on my arms." I showed Dr. Moses.

"They came all of a sudden."

I was smiling. Dr. Moses wasn't.

He moved closer to me and Mom.

He moved in slow motion, like a snake about to strike his prey. When he opened up his mouth, it was as if he were yawning. I felt like I was frozen.

"Well that's why I scheduled this visit Paul," said Dr. Moses, grasping my shoulder.

"Mrs. Christian I need you and Paul to sit down."

Dr. Moses adjusted his tie and cleared his throat. His eyes were so big he looked like someone had surprised him. I didn't know what to expect from him.

"Paul," he said, then took a sharp look at Mom and then looked me in the eye, "Paul you've been diagnosed with Acute Myeloid Leukemia, a form of cancer that is dangerous," explained Dr. Moses.

He continued to stare at me.

Then Dr. Moses placed his hand on my shoulder.

I felt like a 1,000- pound concrete building had fallen on me, crushing me flat, along with ~~my~~ all my hopes and dreams. This had to be a nightmare. What the fuck?! No basketball?! All I heard was no basketball. My dream of playing for the greatest college basketball team in the world was gone. Crushed like an elephant stepping on a grape, a deflated balloon was more like it.

"No!" cried Mom. "What can you do Dr. Moses? Can he take some medicine? Exercise? Eat vegetables? What, what can you do? What can we do? I can't believe this is happening!"

Mom took a deep breath, put her hands in her face and shook her head. She regained her composure, took another deep breath and said firmly, "What are the chances of Paul dying? What is the survival rate of people diagnosed with Acute Myeloid Leukemia? I want all of the information! All of it! I will not lose Paul, too! Do you hear me?"

"Mrs. Christian," said Dr. Moses, "he can survive but it's going to require hard work and chemotherapy-"

"No! That's not what I'm asking Dr. Moses!" said Mom, speaking louder. "What are his chances of living? That's all I'm concerned about!"

Dr. Moses grabbed Mom's hand and said, "He has more than a 50% chance of living but we have to work together as a team. You have to do your part as his parent, making sure he goes to chemotherapy appointments, eating right and getting the proper rest. But **AML** is very dangerous, too. And he could die, too. That's why we have to work together as a team."

The room was spinning and all I could hear was all these muffled voices. Suddenly, everything went dark and memories shot through my mind: when my Dad taught me how to shoot a basketball, Dad taking me to my first NC State basketball game, then me staring at my Dad in his casket. I opened my eyes. I was lying on the floor and I had passed out! Did I already? *I thought to myself.* I tried to stand up, but only to fall back down. My legs wobbled like a new born foal as I slowly stood up.

"No!" I cried out. "This can't be! How can I have cancer or Acute or whatever you call it Dr. Moses? I'm young. I'm strong. I'm a basketball player. Young people don't get sick with cancer and stop playing basketball. Why are you saying this? No! No!"

"Paul, we'll beat this cancer! We'll beat it!" said Mom.

"How are we going to beat it Mom? Tell me how?" I said through tears. "Nobody, and I mean nobody beats Cancer! Nobody beats The BIG C'. Nobody beats his ass! Nobody beats this shit! You see what it did to Dad! And...Everybody else! Why me?" I yelled and sobbed into my mom's chest. "Why! Why!!"

Dr. Moses tried to console me. but I moved away.

"Paul I know you're upset, explained Dr. Moses. "I will help; we will help you get through this. I'll make sure you get the best treatment in the world. You can beat this, but it's going to take time and hard work from all of us!"

"I don't want to die like Dad did, Mom!" "Damn! I'm scared."

"You won't!" said Mom, hugging me tightly. "God will take care of this. It's in his hands."

I hope so. I thought, dropping my head into my hands.

The ride home was the longest ride in the world. Everything moved in slow motion: the cars moved slowly; the stoplights stayed red forever; the birds had slowed down to a speed where I felt I could reach out and touch them; the clouds moved in circles and hovered close to the tree lines; and the wind slowed. But my thoughts were moving at 100 miles an hour. So fast I got a slight headache. Like someone took a sledge hammer to my head. My body was numb, you could've stuck me with a needle and I wouldn't-have felt anything. I figured this is how people feel before they died, numb and all alone. And how could God allow this to happen to an athletic teenager with dreams to play college basketball? I shook my head and the headache got worse, to the point I got nauseated. Even the tears rolled down my face in slow motion. The saddest day in my life was upon me. I felt like a grass hopper trapped in a glass jar full of holes at the top, hopelessly waiting to be released. That's what cancer felt like to me: trapped in your own sick body but waiting for it to go away forever! And I just kept going over and over what Doctor Moses told me: *And you could die, too. That's why we have to work together as a team. What freaking team will work together?* The only team I wanted to be a part of was my basketball team! My Eagles teammates and my coaches. But that wasn't going to happen now. At the time I didn't know it, but I had a long, difficult and treacherous road ahead of me.

When Mom and I walked through the door of our brick house, I ran upstairs to my room, Scooter jumped into my arms, licking my face like crazy. I was so glad to see him, feeling he was the only friend that I had. I fed him some doggie bones and played nerf basketball with him on his miniature goal. I'd toss the nerve ball about four feet in the air, he'd leap up and catch the ball with his slobbery mouth and slam it into the basket and bark! Slam dunk for Scotter! More doggie bones for my buddy! I figured if I played basketball with him my life would magically go back to normal. I could be a teenager again. Live Life. Date the pretty girls. Go to the parties. Just bea damn teenager with no worries. The more I thought about having cancer the more upset I got. Damn my life was screwed. The more I thought about having cancer the madder I got. I put Scooter outside the room. Then all hell broke loose. I stormed down the stairs, out the back door and slammed it hard. I kicked in the tool shed and grabbed an axe. Clutching the axe tightly,I chopped at the small oak tree in the backyard, bark flying off like grenades. I kept swinging until the handle broke. I slung the head of the ax through the window of the shed. The window shattered into a thousand pieces. My eyes flared up as the axe head ripped through the wooden wall. When I saw the ax head stuck in the wall, I took a deep breath, gritted my teeth and unclenched my fist. Then I dropped to my knees and cried.

"My God this sucks! Why can't I stop vomiting?" I screamed out loud. I hugged onto the toilet as my stomach erupted like a volcano, spitting out yellowish and pink vomit. A vice grip had taken hold of my stomach muscles, forcing me to dry heave and spit out nothing but air bubbles. My body rocked back and forth violently, as if my body was getting electrocuted.

Mom burst through the door screaming, "Paul! What's wrong baby? Are you ok?"

"No Mom!" I said, holding my stomach.

"Paul! We have to get you to the doctor. You have vomited everywhere!"

"No Mom! I don't need any doctor! For them to tell me something else is wrong! It's probably that nasty food I'm eating now!"

"Don't be silly Paul! You're going to the Doctor!"

"Please Mom! It's a side effect of taking the medicine!" I said through clinched teeth.

"Remember Dr. Moses told us this! And my weight might drop, too!"

"I'm not taking any chances Paul! I know what Dr. Moses said! I just want you feeling better!"

"Mom I'm hurting badly right now! Can I just go to sleep and we go to the Doctor later! I'm just so tired!" I said as I my head hung on the side of the toilet.

"Fine! Mom said as she stroked my forehead.

I had to tell Mom something so she would leave me alone. My goodness she made having cancer worse. After I assured her I needed some rest, I vomited some more, except I made an effort not to be loud. My stomach felt like a wildfire and could barely breathe. I huffed and puffed as if I were blowing out candles. With no strength to walk, I crawled out of the bathroom at a snail's pace, one hand and one knee at a time. With each movement, my head throbbed and neck sniffed, making me keep it straight! I used the crown of my head to open up my bedroom door, which was slightly open. Pulled myself up by the ends of the bedspread, slid underneath the covers and said a small prayer, asking God why me?

Having cancer brought me so much unwanted attention and special treatment. Everyone feels sorry for you and wants you to know how much they care about you. People would bring me fruit baskets, clothes, tickets to the movie, for sporting events, free food, a free haircut and even meeting girls. I didn't give a damn about any of that! Cancer had taken away all of my joy. And I showed the world what I meant. The hell with cancer and all of its perks! One morning I took one of the many fruit baskets I received and tossed them out of the window, landing in the spot where Scooter poops, then commanded Scooter to poop on it. As soon as someone gave me a pair of shoes, I'd take the laces out and wrap it around the shoe in newspaper and glue and let sit and get hard so Scooter could slob on it and play with it. Or poop on it. It didn't matter to me.

My phone rang constantly. Whenever I received a phone call, I'd answer the phone with a fake voice, hoarse and low as if I were on life support. Coughing, pretending to choke and vomit made people not want to talk to me over the phone. This is how I handled it.

Phone rings

"H-e-l-l-o!" I'd answer very slowly.

"Hey Paul! It's Ruth. How are you doing? Wanted to know if I could bring you   something to eat? Just wanted to see if you were hungry."

"O-k-a-y!" I said slowly, "hold… on… R-u-t-h!"

I stuck my finger down my throat to make me gag. When my bony finger reached the end of my throat, I let out a huge roar as if I had vomited. The roar was so loud I heard Ruth say "Oh God!"

I waited like a few minutes before coming back to the phone. I talked real slow.

"I….m b-a-c-k-k-k Ruth!" I said in a sick tone.

"Oh Paul I'm so sorry you're sick. I'll let you rest and come by another time. Okay?"

"O-k-a-y R-u-t-h!T-h…a…n..k..y-o-u!"

The sick ploy worked every time. But I enjoyed it more whenever someone visited me in person.

Before the person arrived, I would pour warm water all over my body to appear sweaty. Then I proceeded to eat a whole can of beans and cabbage and fart up the room, closing the door tightly so the stink would stay in there. I wanted my room to smell like a filthy garbage dump. That would drive them away. Leave me alone.

Nobody was exempt from my wrath! Or meanness for that matter.

That went for professional people, too, especially over the phone.

"May I speak to Paul Christian?"

"Hello. This is Paul."

"My name is Patricia Laney; I'm the General Manager of *King Movie Theater*. On behalf of myself and the employees we would like to offer you and anyone of your choice one year of free movie passes."

"Thanks so much! I'll love that! Can't wait to receive the tickets and put them on eBay! I'm sure I can make a profit like y'all do!"

"Excuse me!" she said.

"Yeah, I'm going to sell these movies tickets to the highest bidder. Thanks again!" I said.

"Well Paul, we don't want you to sell them! We're preferred that you use them for yourself and a friend or family member," she said.

"So are you saying that you will not give me the tickets? Are you taking the tickets away from a cancer stricken teenager? Wow! I wonder how Channel 11 News will react to this!" I said so humbly.

"Sir, I mean Paul…yes there'll your tickets…just would like for you.. to use them and not sell them. I mean whatever you'll like would be fine…I guess," she said nervously.

"Are you sure Ms. Laney? Because I don't want any hard feelings, especially with a teenager with cancer."

"Oh no not at all!" she said quickly. "No problem at all!"

"Okay! Great! Glad we can do business together!" I said with a wide grin on my face.

"My address is-"

"I already have your address Paul!" she interrupted.

"I'll be looking forward to the tickets! When can I expect them? I'm very anxious!"

"Soon Sir…I mean Paul," she said stuttering. She was definitely scared.

"Okay! Can't wait! Awesome! The sooner I get them the quicker I can sell them and get paid!"

"Yes, whatever you want to do with them Mr. Paul… I mean Paul," she said.

Then I hung up the phone and blocked her number. I felt satisfied.

My coaches and friends weren't exempted either. Coach Gomes came over one day and I pretended to be sleep. Since I knew he was coming over, I stuffed my mouth full of grapes and when he tapped me on the shoulder and said, "Hey buddy! How are you doing? I brought something for you!" I shot straight up and spit out the grapes as if I were vomiting. Coach Gomes jumped back as the grapes covered his white jump suit and red and white sneakers. He jumped back immediately. Then he grabbed a towel and cleaned me up and told me how much he loved me. "I'm definitely praying for you Paul!" said Coach Gomes, squeezing me so hard I could smell his cologne.

"You hang in there buddy! You'll beat this thing and I'm here for you. I'll do whatever I can to help you. Just remember don't ever give up. You will beat this-cancer. I know you're a fighter!"

"Thanks coach," I said through slurred speech. "I appreciate you coming by."

"Anytime Paul!" he said. Then he left, but turned around quickly.

"Oh I almost forgot Paul. Here is a letter from a school. Take care and call me if you need anything."

My ploy didn't work on coach, but I was anxious to read this letter. All of a sudden, I had a burst of energy. Maybe a school wanted me to play for them. I opened up the letter quickly.

NORTH CAROLINA STATE UNIVERSITY BASKETBALL

Dear Paul

Congratulations, you have the opportunity to get a quality education and play exciting college basketball. A University degree from North Carolina State is one the most prestigious in America. As the head basketball coach at the university, I want to formally extend a scholarship to you. My staff and I are committing to helping you develop your skills on the basketball court and off of it. My coaching experiences to coach and teach from all levels, high school, college, and the NBA. You will learn the systems and techniques that have benefitted several players who have gone on to the next level. Life after basketball opportunities are here for you at the North Carolina State University. The North Carolina State experience allows you the outstanding opportunity to earn the letters NBA, M.Ed. or PH.D behind your name. The education you earn lays the foundation for your professional life's work, a necessity in today's competitive workplace.

Game and movie tickets were sent to the highest bidder on eBay. Or I let them stay there on the dresser like an artifact. Or flush them down the toilet.

NCAA rules require me to tell you that for this scholarship to remain available to you, you must meet the following requirements:

A. Successfully complete your senior academic curriculum.

B. Meet all NCAA initial eligibility requirements that apply for your senior academic year.

C. Meet the admission requirements of North Carolina State University.

D. Continue to live by the social rules that made you an outstanding student, athlete and role model in your school and community.

E. Receive the recommendation of your high school coach.

Mt. Sinai basketball has a winning tradition. We want you to help us win the conference championships and an opportunity to win a National Championship.

I want you on my team! Good luck to you and the entire Eagles basketball family this season.

Sincerely

Malachi Abraham

Oh my goodness! I shouted. I couldn't believe it. I received a scholarship to play basketball. It was college basketball. I was so excited I jumped up and down on the bed like a kid. I jumped so high I hit my head on the ceiling. That was best news ever. I couldn't wait to tell Mom. But Mom busted through like a bull!

"Paul are you alright! What's wrong! Are you okay?" Mom said excitedly, rubbing my face.

"Mom! I got a basketball scholarship! Can you believe it oh man?" I screamed out as I bear hugged Mom!

"I did it Mom!"

"Wow! Really! Oh my God! That's….that's awesome Paul! This is unbelievable!" Mom yelled with full of excitement.

She was so excited she jumped on the bed with me. We jumped up and down like little kids at the park.

"Paul this is the best news you could receive!" said Mom.

"I know it is Mom!"

"What's the name of the school?" she asked.

"N.C. State baby!" I screamed

"The Wolfpack! Oh my God the Wolfpack! You'll be playing for the Wolfpack!" she screamed.

Mom hugged me so hard; I thought I was being hugged by a fat girl. And then she kissed me on my cheek. Then she jumped off of the bed and ran out of the room.

"What's wrong Mom!" I said as I ran behind her.

"Nothing Paul," she said as she ran into her room and locked the door.

What could possibly be wrong with her I thought? As I approached her door, I heard sobbing. I knocked as loud as I could and rapidly turned the doorknob. But Mom never answered. I knocked on the door again. But I would get my answer soon.

Suddenly, it hit me in my stomach like a karate chop. I knew where the tears came from! I still have cancer. That's why Mom was crying. She figured I wouldn't be able to play basketball. My goodness. Reality struck me again. I really did have cancer. And it wasn't going anywhere!

The next morning I started my chemotherapy treatment at Duke Hospital. I was in the worse mood ever because I had cancer and it was somebody's fault. I even blamed God. *Why me God! Am I not good enough I thought?*

And Mom made it worse talking to me en route to the hospital.

"How are you Paul?" Mom asked, kissing me on my forehead.

I didn't say anything. I sat there for a minute angry.

"Paul!" she said

"I'm fine Mom!" I snapped.

Mom paused for a few minutes. Then she took a deep breath.

"Okay Paul," she said softly, "I know you're not in the best of mood, but I'll get better. You just have to do the things the Doctor says you're supposed to do. And the Doctors say-it's treatable and you have a good chance of living. So that's great Paul!"

"Great for whom?" I snapped. "I'm the one with cancer and feeling sick all of the time. I'm the one who's missing out on my Senior year of high school. I'm the one not playing basketball! I'm the one who's missing the prom. No girlfriend! Not able to meet girls! No parties! No hanging out with friends! No nothing but this stupid cancer that has ruined my life! Damn! My young life is screwed Mom! It's freaking screwed!"

I jumped out the car and slammed the door.

Mom ran behind me and grabbed my hand. I snatched it away until she regained her grip and pulled me to her. "Listen Paul, this isn't easy for me either. It's killing me inside, too. You're my only child. My only child. I don't want you to die. I stay up all night praying and asking

God to cure you. I've cried so much that I can't cry anymore. I'm doing everything I can to help you. I refuse to lose you. I'm not going to sit back and watch you die like your….-"

"Like Dad!" I said

"Yes...like your father!" she said slowly.

"Why did he have to pass cancer to me?" I said angrily. "It's not fair and selfish."

"Paul! You're going to win this battle. You have to have faith." Pleaded Mom.

"I lost my faith a long time ago." I said.

"Paul,"-

I waved my hand to stop Mom. I wasn't in the mood to hear about God and having faith.

Deep down I felt bad for Mom because she had to put her life on hold to take care of me. But I didn't want to be a charity case, even if I were her son. I saw how Mom struggled when Dad had cancer. I saw the pain in her face, the sleepless nights taking care of Dad, losing weight, not having an appetite, and most of all, never having time for me. We grew distance during those times because of her taking care of Dad 24/7. The memories were so painful a migraine came about.

When we entered the Doctor's office, it reminded me of a combat zone with all of the children and teenagers wearing scarfs, in wheelchairs, coughing, crying or just lying in their mother's lap. I was amazed at how most of them were calm, reading books, playing with toys or talking to each other. Although they had experienced pain, they were dealing with it, something I didn't understand. I guess they had accepted their fate. I immediately felt out of place as a 6'5 giant who was trying to fit in, but of course I wasn't. As I stared in amazement, my name was called.

"Hello Ms. Christian and Paul," said the nurse. "Go to room 316. Dr. John is waiting for you."

"Thank you," said Mom.

I didn't say anything. I took the long, slow walk down the corridor as if I were going to the electric chair. My size 18 shoes kept tripping over each other, prompting Mom to keep asking if I were alright. *Heck no I wasn't alright!, I remembered thinking.* I was scared as hell and was putting up a brave front for Mom, even though I showed my angry outbursts. The pictures on the wall of smiling, bald headed children whose cancer was in remission gave me some hope my chemo appointment would be okay.

Dr. John's office resembled a museum with huge paintings of famous Presidents and historical figures, like Dr. Martin Luther King, Gandhi, Mother Theresa and Winston Churchill. In the corner of his office, miniature statues of Julius Caesar of Rome, Egyptian Queen Cleopatra, and Greek philosophers Socrates, Plato, and Aristotle. The furniture was dark blue and gigantic, as if Giants were supposed to sit here. I settled down on the black and blue leather recliner, surrounded by medical magazines and fluffy pillows with a Blue Devils emblem. A dish of tiny Hersey bars rested on the arm chair. The aroma of medicine and air freshener made my nostrils tingle. Soft classical music vibrated throughout the office. The sound of wind chimes relaxed my nerves, reminding me of the times Dad and I went fishing. The combination of classical music and wind chimes had me daydreaming. I placed my "beats" headphones over my ears and leaned back in the recliner. Music from rapstar Drake blasted through my ears. I smiled down at the red spots on my arm. I felt relieved for some reason. I took a deep breath and popped a Hersey in my mouth and waited for the doctor.

Before I knew it, I had dozed off and Mom nudged me because I started to snore. And I snored hard.

"Paul! Snapped Mom.
"Sorry." I said
"I know you're tired, but I don't want you snoring like a locomotive train," joked Mom.
"I know Mom," laughing.

Mom had a way of making me laugh when I'm in a bad mood. For a moment, the laughter made me forget why I was there. But when a tall, lean man with broad shoulders called my name, I remembered why I was there.

"Hello Paul," said Dr. John, extending his large hand. "I'm the Medical Oncologist who will be treating you. So how are you doing this morning? It's good to meet you and Mrs. Christian."

"Hello Dr. John," I said, looking at his receding hairline. I went back into my bad mood.

And Dr. John wasted no time explaining my chemo treatment. He assured Mom and I Chemo was very effective. It had a high success rate. Of course, Mom had a boatload of questions. Heck, I thought she was the one getting chemo treatment.

"So explain the drugs again? I want to be clear on what it does," asked Mom.

"Sure Ms. Christian," said Dr. John, very kindly. "The drugs are called Cytostatic, which objective is to stop cancer cells from continuing to divide uncontrollably. It's very effective."

"How long the effect of the administered drug lasts?" asked Mom? "How much time the body needs to recover?And the overall length of treatment?."

"Mom! I said, Could you stop- " Dr. John cut me off.

"We'll be using Curative chemotherapy. It aims to eliminate all cancer cells from the body to achieve a permanent cure. This gives Paul the best opportunity to be healthy."

"That's great," said Mom smiling. "I'll ask you the other questions later Dr. John. I know Paul has to go and get this done. Thank you Dr. John."

"You're very welcome Ms. Christian. Feel free to always ask me questions and there is cancer literature you can read up on while you wait for Paul."

"Thanks again," said Mom. "Love you Paul. It's going to be okay, you'll strong!"

Then Mom held my hand and planted a kiss on my forehead.

"Love you, too!" I said as I slowly released her hand.

I followed Dr. John down the long hallway. I felt like it was a death walk, a walk to the electric chair. For the first time, I was really scared, so scared that I stopped, pivoted and turned half way around before Dr. John asked me a random question.

"So Paul, what is your height? And whose your favorite basketball team?" asked Dr. John

"I'm. I'm…6'6 sir," I stuttered, "and I'm a Wolfpack fan. Die hard Wolfpack fan."

"So am I! How awesome," said Dr. John excitedly. Then he gave me a high five and ushered me into the chemotherapy room.

Sitting inside the chemo room were the prettiest nurses I'd ever seen. They had to be Super Models. My goodness they were gorgeous. One was Black and the other White. Long eyelashes accompanied them with a set of shiny brown eyes and a shapely toned body had me starstruck. I fumbled the keys in my pockets, twisted the ring on my finger and swallowed hard. Mouth became dry and I mumbled my name and dropped my head when they spoke. Maybe they placed these gorgeous women here to ease my mind.

"Hello Paul!" they said at the same time.

"Hello," I said sheepishly. I know I had to look like a tall duffus, talking all shy and stuff

They calmed my nerves when the white nurse held my hand and said, "It's going to be okay Paul," she said calmly.

Dr. John and his gorgeous nurses explained the procedure and what they were going to do. They checked my vitals and all that good stuff before we got started.

"Is it going to hurt?" I asked

"Let's hope not, but we're going to put this needle into your vein and you'll feel a pinch,"said the gorgeous black nurse. "Let us know if you feel a burning sensation or any long lasting pain."

"Okay! I'm ready," I said.

I sat patiently as the gorgeous nurse stuck the needle in my arm. For some reason, I never felt the needle go into my vein. So I leaned back and listened to 2Pac's "All Eyez On Me". His music relaxed me and took my mind off of things like cancer. 2Pac was a 90's rapper who was shot and died seven days later. I wasn't born when he died, but my Dad introduced me to him at a young age. And I fell in love with his music.2Pac was ahead of this time, I guess a rebel with a cause, a revolutionary rapper. I identified with him more than ever because I was fighting cancer.

As I sat there listening to "All Eyez On Me," I felt a warm sensation and nodded off. I dreamt I played a basketball game called *horse* with NBA superstar LeBron James. In the dream, I did an acrobatic dunk, jumping high and taking the ball between the legs and slam dunked the ball. LeBron did the exact same dunk but did a 360 in midair and slam dunked. Let's just say LeBron won the game of Horse. Then I heard a distant voice say, "Paul! Hey Paul! Are you okay? How are you feeling?" Then I felt a nudge and woke up. The White, gorgeous nurse wanted to know if felt any pain and how was I feeling overall.

"I'm good. Very good," I mumbled.

"That's good to know," she smiled. "You're almost done."

"Really?"I asked.

"Yeah," she said.

"That was fast," I said.

"Time flies when you fall asleep," she joked.

"Of course!" I laughed.

Man I wished I were older because I'd definitely ask her out. The thought of having cancer didn't seem so bad after all if these pretty nurses could take care of me. But having a girlfriend was almost impossible. What teenage girl wanted a teenage boy with cancer? None was my opinion. The thought of it saddened me.

Then both nurses appeared with Dr. John and nurse took the needle out of my arm. This time it was the black nurse.

"How do you feel buddy? Asked Dr. John. "Here is a bottle of water."

"Thank you," I said. "I feel lightheaded and thirsty, that's about it. And I'm hungry."

"Okay. One of the side effects of chemotherapy is feeling light headed or fatigue and being thirsty are just a few. There are many more in this pamphlet I'll be giving you."

By this time, Mom had entered the room, kissing on me like I was a new born baby.

"Hey baby," said Mom, rubbing my forehead. "How are you feeling? Are you hungry? I brought you a subway sandwich, steak and cheese with bell peppers, tomatoes, onions, mustard with oil and vinegar and some chips. And some water."

"Thanks Mom," I said shyly. It felt weird talking to Mom with the gorgeous nurses staring at me.

"Yes, I'm starving. Thanks again Mom," I said.

I took the steak and cheese sub from Mom and let her talk to Dr. John and the nurses. But I couldn't eat my sandwich right away because Dr. John wanted to talk to Mom and I together. Couldn't this wait, I thought. I was starving.

"Here is a schedule of chemotherapy appointments and make sure you follow the recommended diet. Get plenty of rest, drink plenty of fluids, and if you have the energy, you can do some leisurely walking. Avoid getting an infection and always eat freshly cooked food and avoid raw meat, fish, eggs, soft cheese and take out foods. Since you're a young man Paul, and if you want to attend a social event, or party for that matter, check with us to see whether your treatment can be arranged so that you are between chemotherapy treatments for that week. Those are the main sticking points; the rest is in the literature I'm giving you. And a prescription." He said.

"Okay thanks a lot Dr. John," I said quickly. I wanted to beat Mom to the punch. "And can I play basketball. Can I go slam dunk? Play some pickup basketball? Play horse?" I joked.

"Of course you can Paul," laughed Dr. John. "You know you can't play any basketball yet. Just take it easy and do some walking. But as you feel better, you can pick up a basketball and try to play or dunk, which you probably can't anyway."

He laughed harder.

"Seriously, I'm joking, but I want you to take it easy, okay buddy. Want you healed."

"You don't have to worry about that Dr. John. I'm going to take great care of him as if he's a baby," said Mom, kissing me again.

"Alright Mom, I'm not a baby," I said.

Dr. John and Mom laughed.

"I have some more information for you Paul .Here is more information for a support group you can attend. There is other information in there that will help you cope and keep your mind off of cancer. It's a long journey, but if you utilize the resources, continue the chemo treatments, take the medication, get plenty of rest, and eat properly, you'll beat cancer. Remember to keep a positive attitude."

"That's awesome. Great words of encouragement," said Mom. "This will really help Paul."

I rolled my eyes. What in the hell was I going to do in a support group, I thought to myself.

"Yes, you're absolutely right Dr. John A positive attitude combined with these resources will definitely help me." I said, pretending to agree with him.

"I'm going to do my best Dr. John." I said.

"I know you will Paul," said Dr. John.

"He sure will," said Mom.

Before Mom and I left, I asked Dr. John a question.

"Dr. John, can the nurses come take care of me? I'm going to need their help. I don't believe Mom can do this by herself." I joked.

Dr. John laughed.

"I'm afraid not Paul. The nurses work here, but feel free to call and ask them questions," he said with a smile.

"Alright, alright," I said smiling. "I thought I'll give it a try."

Mom and I told Dr. John good bye and Mom promised she would take good care of me.

On the ride home, Mom told me how much she loved me and how she took a leave of absence to tend to me. She talked about how she had an itinerary for me and so forth. She talked so much I dozed off, snoring like a freight train as she likes to tell it.

Mom stopped by the local drug store to pick up my meds while I slept in the car. When I woke up, I felt very tired but I noticed a shiny object in the corner of the dashboard. It was a silver and gray folder with a group of teenagers in a circle smiling at a man in the middle of the circle. The folder had a white angel on the cover with a huge cross in the background with a statute of Jesus looking down. I opened up the folder and it was the support group Dr. John had mentioned. I didn't want to go to any support group, only to be around the sick and the shut in. Or the soon to be dead. That's what I heard about cancer groups anyway. I mean really, why would anyone want to sit around and talk about a disease and how it affected you? How it made you feel? How you might die? If you were going to die? I shook my head in disbelief. By this time, Mom had returned with my meds.

"I have to take all of that doggone medicine?" I said. I opened up the bottles and they were big white horse pills. I swear they were the size of my hand. They were made for a whale.

"My goodness," I moaned. "This is going to make me puke!"

"You have to take it Paul," pleaded Mom.

"You have to take it Paul," mocking Mom.

"Paul!" said Mom, placing her hands over my lips.

I knew Mom was serious. Whenever she got serious, I listened. Because she knew how to put the fear of God in me.

"I see you've been reading the Support Group material. What do you think about it? I believe you'll like it and it'll be worth it. You'll need an outlet Paul, something that will not make you depressed or angry. I'm going to do what's best for you, even if you don't think so. You'll thank me later." Mom said.

"Mom I just want to go to sleep," I said.

"Okay," she said. "One more thing Paul, I've talked to my friend Mary about you volunteering at the Wildlife Shelter once you feel better. Since you want to be a veterinarian, I believe this will be a great experience for you."

"Alright Mom, I appreciate that," I said. "And Thanks."

She proceeded to drive us home. The longest drive ever because I became nauseated. I would learn to deal with it, however.

I volunteered at the Wildlife Rehabilitation Center a week later. I loved Mom's friend Mary because when I was younger, she'd let me listen to rap music and stay up all hours of the night. Actually, Mary was my God Mother, but I didn't see her as a God Mother. I saw her more as a Big sister who spoiled her little brother. I couldn't wait to see her, either.

When we saw each other, she hugged me so hard I could feel her heart beat.

"Paul! Paul! Oh my Big Baby looks like a grown man now!" she said loudly. "I'm here for you Paul! You're going to enjoy volunteering here. I know how much you love animals. What a great opportunity to ease your mind."

"You're absolutely right Mary," I said. "This will ease my mind and allow me to focus on getting better in the long run."

"Yes it will, my baby!" she said as she hugged me again.

"Paul, I would've been there for your first chemotherapy appointment but you know I was-"

"I know you were burying your father." I said softly. "I know how much you loved your father. That's where you were supposed to be. I had Mom."

"I know but you're special to me and I just…wanted to be there to show you I care," she said.

"It's okay. I love you still," I said. "You're looking out for me now, so it's all good." We hugged each other again with a long embrace.

Then Mary proceeded to introduce me to everyone and show me around the center. I felt like a rock star with all of the attention I received. The staff offered me food, drinks and $100 dollar gift cards from local stores. I received tons of movie tickets, concert tickets, football tickets to Carolina Panthers games, and basketball tickets to see the NC State Wolfpack. They even gave me toys!

"You're such a brave man! Keep up the fight Paul!" said one lady. "Wow you're tall. Thanks for coming to help," said another lady. "Appreciate your help and keep up the good fight!" said an old man. "Thank you all! Appreciate everything!" I said.

Mary showed me the animals and what my responsibilities were and showed me all of the animals. They had all types of animals, from stray dogs to iguanas to birds, even had some boa constrictors. Excitement came upon me, especially when I saw the stray dogs. I thought about Scooter. I immediately liked the Wildlife Rehabilitation Center. But then something happened that would change me forever.

Whenever I felt nauseated, I'd walk to the Wildlife Rehabilitation Center for some exercise. The long walk made me feel better for some reason, and it beats swallowing those nasty horse pills. Plus, I cleared my mind of having cancer. I'd think about other things, like playing basketball for NC State Wolfpack.

But one day at the Wildlife Rehabilitation Center, I saw a young boy with a bald head wearing a pink NC State shirt, tending to a bird with a broken wing. The young boy wrapped some pink tape around the bird's wing. He seemed so interested in what he was doing; I was curious and introduced myself.

"Hey little man my name is Paul Christian!" I said, extended my hand. "What are you doing?"

"I'm trying to fix the bird's wing. He injured it somehow, but I'm going to make it work so he can fly again," said the young boy.

Was he going to make the bird fly? He could be no more than 10 or 11 years old!

"Well I'm learning how to nurture animals back to health. This is a sparrow. He'll fly again because God takes care of everything that He has created."

He sounded like Mom. I was a loss for words. This kid had leukemia and was smiling and nurturing sparrows. 'Why didn't I have his attitude?'

"And my name is Jericho Walls," he said, finally shaking my hand. "Wow! You're so tall and you have big hands! Let me guess, you're a basketball player! Right!"

"Yes I am, I said.

"Who is your favorite college basketball team?" he asked.

"N.C. State Wolfpack! All day every day!" I said with a big smile on my face. "And it looks like you're a Wolfpack fan, too!"

"Absolutely! I love the Wolfpack. I'm a die-hard Wolfpack fan!" he said excitedly. He jumped up and gave me a high five.

"I get to go to all of their games, too. My Mother gets the tickets from some high person at N.C. State who looks out for kids like me who have Leukemia. I forgot the name of the program. It's the same program that lets me come here and treat birds," he said.

"That's very nice of N.C. State," I said.

"I want to be an Ornithologist and a Veterinarian when I grow up," I'm going to study at N.C. State University when I grow up."

"What is an Ornithologist?" I asked. "And I want to be a veterinarian too, Jericho."

"An Ornithologist is a wildlife biologist who studies birds. I want to study birds then learn how to operate on them if they get sick or break a wing. This is what I'm learning right now. Ms. Ruth is teaching me," said Jericho.

"That's great. You'll make a good Ornithologist and Veterinarian," I said. "Just keep working hard."

"It was nice to meet you, but my group is about to leave. You can always come visit me at the hospital and I'll let you see the rest of my birds."

"What hospital?" I asked.

"UNC Children's Hospital," said an older woman wearing a UNC Volunteer badge. I guess it was Ms. Ruth.

"Yes, UNC Hospital," he said with a frown. "You know I hate the Tar Heels being an N.C. State Wolfpack fan."

"Trust me I know how you feel buddy!" I said.

"You can come anytime to volunteer. We need all the help we can get. The kids like teenagers," said Ms. Ruth.

"Thanks!" I said. "I'll do that."

"By the way, I'm Ruth," she said, extending her hand.

"I'm Paul Christian, nice to meet you Ms. Ruth," I said.

"Please come by," said Jericho. "I need all of the Wolfpack people there to help fight the UNC fans."

"Okay," I said with a chuckle.

We shook hands and I promised him that I would come visit him. That particular day was awesome because I felt like I had found a new friend, even though he was only 12 years old.

All of a sudden I had goose bumps. Finally, I had something to smile about.

I attended the Cancer Support Group two days later. I wanted to call it cancer camp because everyone was there for a one specific reason, just like kids would attend a basketball camp or football camp with a purpose in mind. Except here, we all had a deadly disease that could kill all of us, or be a constant reminder it could kill us at any time. Amazing how this Cancer Group would be nothing but a constant reminder I can die or will die. I shook my head of the situation as Mom dropped me off in the front of the building.

As I climbed the huge, steep steps, I recognized there were a lot of teenagers there with cancer. Some of them were very young and some of them were my age. The younger children looked like cute babies who didn't have a care in the world. When I found my assigned room, there were about 10 people in there already sitting on these pink cushion stools in a large circle. A mural of Jesus and his disciples was on a massive wall in the back of the room. The sign in sheet was located on a pink wooden table surrounded by cancer literature. The smell of Welch's grape juice and Oreo cookies filled the room. Bowls of pineapple, strawberries, and grapes sat on a silver and pink tray outlined with pink napkins.

I grabbed a bowl of pineapples and some Welch's juice. I took my seat and ate my cookies. I looked around as people were in their own clicks having conversation. I hoped this group session wasn't a cliquish thing like high school. A few more people walked in after me. Then once everyone was seated, the group leader, Matthew, introduced himself and told us how his cancer was in remission. He told us his cancer was in remission. Carcinoma was diagnosed a few years back and beat it. He said he found comfort with a support group. Matthew explained his story of how he was a former college football star. His broad shoulders and muscular arms were sculpted like a body builder. Matthew looked like the WWE wrestler and movie star "Rock." He said having cancer derailed his dreams of playing professional football. However, he was content because he identified his true calling. His true calling was being a counselor, a counselor who helps cancer patients, to help them succeed and overcome the dreaded disease of cancer.

He explained the group rules and stuff and how we should use this as an outlet, a resource to benefit us. We were encouraged to introduce ourselves, talk about ourselves, our interests, goals and talk about our cancer. Basically, the Support Group was something to be positive, uplifting each other with this deadly disease called Cancer.

I liked it so far because there were all races of people there and age groups. There were young children there, too, which surprised me. I realized everyone and anyone could get cancer.

Matthew passed around a basket full of skinny strips of white paper and told everyone to take one. Each piece of paper had a number on it. The person with the highest number had to introduce themselves first and go from there, but only if they felt like it.

A young girl stood up to introduce herself first. She had to be about 13 years of age. "Hello everyone! My name is Ruth," she said. "I'm 14 years old I and I was diagnosed with Hodgkin Lymphoma a few months ago. I go to chemotherapy appointments and I'm finally learning to deal with having cancer. It was very hard at first because I couldn't do anything with my friends. After chemo treatments, I feel better and this group really helps. I'm getting stronger. That's all!"

"That's awesome and thanks for sharing Ruth," said Matthew. "Let's all clap and give Ruth a standing ovation and tell her 'thank you for being brave.'" We all stood up and clapped and said, "thank you for being brave!"

I learned that was the routine after someone introduced themselves. The next person to go up was another female named Ester. She was 19 years of age and described her daily struggle with bone cancer. She wore a white bandanna with red and white crosses. She said her faith in God keeps her going. She said her radiation treatments made her tired but would keep up the good fight.

"In order to beat cancer, you have to have a positive attitude!" said Ester. Everyone stood up and clapped.

Three more people went before me. They were all teenagers. As they spoke, I thought about what I was going to say, how cancer has affected my life, and all of that good stuff. I still felt robbed of my health and young life with cancer, so I harbored some anger and resentment, especially those that were either cancer free or whose cancer was in remission.

Before I introduced myself, I wrote down what I was going to say and put on a phony smile, that way it would be over quickly. I stood up and opened up my notepad and said, "Hello good people. My name is Paul Christian and I have acute myeloid leukemia and I had my first chemo treatment last week. And having cancer sucks. Thank you." I said quickly.

Before I could sit down, and before anyone clapped, everyone started asking me all types of questions.

"How tall are you?" asked a young boy. "And do you play basketball?"

"What did you think of the chemo treatments?" asked another

"What scares you the most about having leukemia?" asked Ester

"Do you have a girlfriend?" joked, a boy wearing sunglasses. He looked familiar for some reason.

"Well yes, I do play basketball…I mean I used to play basketball…I'm not playing basketball right now because of AML. Chemo treatments were okay or blah. What scares me is dying. I don't want to die and I hate having AML because it screwed up my life. No, I have no girlfriend and I'm not looking for one."

There was a brief silence. Then there were more questions. That shocked me because I knew my anger was showing. But that's what I thought.

"Where do you go for your treatments?" blurted someone.

"Just keep a positive attitude and you will overcome leukemia," said one female, who had the prettiest voice I'd ever heard. Then the boy wearing the sunglasses said, "How do you feel about the Wolfpack basketball this year Paul? And do you eat your vegetables?" he said laughing.

I looked closer but didn't recognize him right away. He took off his glasses and said, "It's me! Jericho,from the Wildlife Rehabilitation Center." Wow! I couldn't believe he was here.

"Hey Jericho!" I said excitedly. "Glad to see you."

"This is awesome, to see two group members interact in harmony," said Matthew. "This is an excellent time to make a transition to you Jericho."

"My name is Jericho Walls and I'm thirteen years old. I'm still taking chemo treatments for Acute Lymphoblastic Leukemia. I like to call it the **All disease.** I have one more chemo treatment before I'm done. Chemo treatments aren't really fun, but I feel great because I get to work on the sparrows at the Wildlife Rehab Center," he said. As soon as he said that, everyone said, "Birdman! Birdman!" Jericho smiled and showed his pearly white teeth.

"I love the Sparrows. The best feeling is helping an animal recover from a devastating injury. In a lot ways, that's what cancer is. It takes over your body and hurts you, but there is stuff like chemotherapy, medicine and doctors that will help put you back together in one piece. "To make you better". I know I'm helping the Sparrows get better. It takes my mind off of having cancer. But my faith comes from God," said Jericho.

The group erupted with a mixture of clapping and chants of "Amen! Amen! Birdman! Birdman! Birdman!" Even Matthew joined in the chorus. "Amen! Birdman! Birdman!" "What a positive attitude to have Jericho!" said Matthew.

Jericho was one popular kid, and he was wise beyond his years. To be his age and speak so clearly and thoughtful, was astounding. Here I was almost eighteen years old and had a bad attitude about cancer and life. Hearing him talk was enlightening, I thought to myself.

"Does anyone have any questions for Jericho?" asked Matthew. Everyone raised their hands into the air. Jericho answered questions like a well-spoken politician.

"Jericho where do you get your positive attitude from?" asked a group member named Julie.

"You can either let cancer beat you or you can beat cancer. I decided to beat cancer rather than let cancer beat me and take away my spirit. There's a choice in this matter. We do have a choice: It's either get killed by the 'Boogie Man', which is cancer, or be the Super Hero and kill it. I chose to be the Super Hero, because I want to live and grow up and live a productive life" said Jericho.

"Amen to that!" shouted the group.

"I hear you," said another.

"My faith is in God, Jesus Christ is my savior," added Jericho.

Everyone asked him a question and he answered their questions, too, in an adult like manner. I sat there in awe at how this skinny and short teenager captivated the group like Michael Jackson rocked a concert. Or more like a mixture of Taylor Swift and Justin Bieber. I couldn't believe what I was witnessing. This was unreal.

Then someone nudged me and said, "You know Jericho is like a genius. He's gifted. He can play all types of instruments, speaks different languages, and a math wizard. He's in the 10th grade, too, said a guy named Curtis.

"Wow! That's amazing," I said. Then I decided to ask him a question.

"Do you worry about dying? Does the thought of dying of cancer keep you up at night?" I asked.

"No I never think about dying Paul. It never crosses my mind because if I focus on death, then cancer wins. Cancer has defeated me. We were all born to die, to die at some point in our life's lives. There is an expiration date for all of us. So why ponder on death? It's going to happen regardless, regardless if you have cancer or not. Just because we have an ailment that can kill us, doesn't mean it will kill us. Cancer is just another form of death, another entity, if you will. No need to worry about something that's going to naturally happen anyway, whether I'm thirteen or 113 years old."

The room erupted again.

"Do you worry about dying Paul?" asked Jericho.

"Yes I do. I try not to think about it. I try to focus on other things like playing basketball or pretending not having it at all, but it's hard!" I said.

"I understand but remember it's a choice in how we handle it. You have to ask yourself do you want to be the Super Hero or get killed by the Boogie Man? Treat cancer like playing a video game *'Assassins Creed'*. You kill the enemy because you want to live another day," said Jericho.

"Interesting!"I said. I sounded like I was listening to a younger version of Joel Osteen, the popular television Evangelist. A teenage prodigy wise beyond his years. This kid was definitely special.

Because of time constraints, Matthew couldn't allow more questions and we ended the group with a prayer written by Jericho. "Dear Lord, I ask you to give everyone in this room the strength, knowledge, understanding, positive attitude, determination, and favor from You to carry on. I ask you God to allow all of us to think of positive things and not negative things as we go through this journey with you by our sides. God make us the leader not the follower, the head not the tail, and the lender not the borrower. Just continue to give us the strength and walk with us on this path because we know you're with us all of the way! Amen!"

All of us congratulated Jericho on his prayer. Although I didn't understand everything in his prayer, I felt relieved for some reason. I found Jericho outside. When caught up to him, he was talking to the prettiest girl ever. My goodness, I thought at the time. She was GORGEGOUS! Absolutely stunning. She had long black, shiny hair. Her eyes were hazel green, lips full, arched eye brows with high cheeks bones that gave way to her honey colored complexion. She wore a black dress, one inch Leopard print heels, and a pair of brown tear drop earrings. Her necklace fell right above her belly button, bearing a silver cross. Silver bangles hung off her wrist; you could hear them when she moved her arms. Her Leopard Clutch purse and big face silver watch represented the look of a Cover Girl Model. This young woman was something out of a magazine.

I was never the shy type to talk to a girl. If I liked a girl, I made it known. But this girl right here was out of my league, it seemed. She probably had a boyfriend. I know she wouldn't talk to guy with cancer. Heck, the best I could do was getting a hello and keep it moving. Pretty girls like her dealt either with rich boys or bad boys. Or both. There was no middle ground with them.

So I paced the pavement back and forth and thought of something to say to Jericho. If I talked to Jericho long enough, maybe she would jump into the conversation. I took a deep breath and fumbled with the Chap Stick in my pocket and thought of something to say. I strolled slowly to give my confidence, but I was a nervous wreck, twisting the Chap Stick on and off. As I got closer, I noticed she had dropped her bracelet. I went from strolling to running to pick up her bracelet. I know I would get a conversation now.

I picked up the bracelet so fast I almost fell. "Excuse me, is this your bracelet?" I asked.

"Yes! Oh thank you so much. I didn't even realize I lost it. I would've been a total wreck when I realized I didn't have it," she said excitedly.

"You're very welcome. Glad I could help!" I said. "I know females love their silver bangles," I said jokingly.

"You're right about that," she said. "I paid a lot of money for this bangle."

"Well I'm sure you can afford it being a model and everything. What magazine do you model for?" I asked jokingly.

"Oh I model for Cosmopolitan Magazine, Glamour Girl Sports Illustrated," she said.

Oh my God just as I thought. She was a model. I knew I was right. Now I was embarrassed.

"Yes that's awesome!" I said, trying to conceal my excitement. "Way to go! Must be nice." I sounded utterly ridiculous now.

"Would you like an autograph?" she asked

"Sure!" I said. "Of course!"

Then she smiled and started laughing.

"I'm no model, far from it," she laughed. "I couldn't resist the temptation. You fell right into it."

We both laughed. "And you must be a comedian," I said laughing. "That was a good joke, very funny. Well you should be a model because you definitely look like one."

"Thank you so much. That's a nice compliment, I must say," she said.

"You are very welcome," I said. "By the way, I'm Paul Christian."

Before she could respond, someone said, "Ezra!"

"Hey Jericho! I can speak for myself!" she said while laughing. "My name is Ezra Walls."

I didn't make the immediate connection because I was staring at her pretty face as if she were a statue. In fact, I had forgotten all about Jericho. By now Jericho had turned around and his attention was on me.

"Ezra, I would like to actually introduce you to Paul, my new friend I met at the Wildlife Rehabilitation Center. Ezra meet Paul, Paul meet Ezra," said Jericho.

"We already met Jericho," said Ezra laughing.

"Yes we did meet," I said smiling.

"Yeah but it wasn't through me," said Jericho laughing. "It has to go through me, and Paul I have to protect my big sister. I normally screen any man that talks to her."

"Your sister!" I repeated.

"Yes, I'm his older sister," said Ezra. "He thinks he's my Dad and tries to tell me what I can and cannot do," she said shaking her head. "He's always joking around and playing pranks."

"Jericho is a bright young man," I said happily. I was thrilled that I knew Jericho. He had a very beautiful sister. Hopefully, I would see her again, maybe several more times.

"He's one special young man. He has a great attitude," I said.

"He sure does. He keeps everyone laughing and in good spirits, never letting us gets down because of him having cancer," she said.

"That's the only way to be," said Jericho.

"Wait a minute," said Ezra, "is this the guy Paul you were telling the family about the other day Jericho? Is this the guy who is supposed to visit you at the UNC Hospital?"

"Yes, Ezra. This is the basketball Giant I told you all about. He loves animals, too," said Jericho.

"That's awesome. Thanks for taking the time to go over to the UNC Hospital. Jericho and the rest of the kids will love it," said Ezra. "Well we better be going."

"Do we have to go right now?" asked Jericho. "It's very early, plus I'm hungry. Can we go got get something to eat? And can Paul join us? I have money."

She paused for a minute, but it seemed like an hour. "Alright we can go. If Paul wants to go, he can come."

I was so excited I got stomach cramps. I could've done 20 back flips and then jumped off of the church steeple. I hid my excitement and pretended to think it over because I didn't want to look desperately. Since she was a 100 on a scale of 10, I wanted to remain calm and play it off as if I talk to pretty girls all the time.

"Hold one second. Let me make sure I have enough time," I said, trying to remain calm. I stalled time by pretending to text Mom. Mom was already in the parking lot, but I wanted to appear like I had a busy schedule and was fitting them into it. Well actually, I was pretending to put her in it. I was going to spend time with Jericho regardless.

"Yeah, I can go and I will meet you all over there. Where are we going?" I asked.

"Israel's Pizza," said Jericho.

"Cool," I said. "I'll be there in 15 minutes."

"Alright," they both said.

I ran to the car and told Mom the good news."Mom! Mom! You're not going to believe I just met the prettiest girl ever. This girl is awesome!" I said excitedly. "And I'm going to eat with her and her brother Jericho! Yes! Yes! I have to make this opportunity count."

"Very Nice Paul! Wow! I'm surprised to see you so happy!" said Mom

"I...I...I...don't know what to say. Where are you all going to eat?" said Mom

"Israel's Pizza," I said.

"Not too far from here," said Mom."A five-minute drive, if that."

"You mind taking me Mom?" I asked.

"Of course not!" Mom said

"Thanks Mom!" I said. I sprayed on some "Boss" cologne and put some mints in my mouth.

"I'm good to go now Mom," I said. "I'm going to make great impression. If I smell good, then I feel good, and when I feel good, I look good."

"You always look good Paul! You're good looks will attract any woman," said Mom.

"Come on Mom!" I said. "You're supposed to feel that way because you're my Mom. I might be ugly to other girls Mom."

Mom laughed. "You're far from ugly. Just look at all of these females who have texted me or called my house looking for you," said Mom, trying to prove her point.

"Whatever Mom, You will say anything to make me feel good," I said laughing.

"It's the truth," said Mom, laughing, too. "You're very handsome."

We drove to Israel's Pizza and I rehearsed a script in my head on what I was going to say to Ezra. I knew I didn't want to be boring or acting like some geek or worse some guy that's never seen a pretty girl. So to break the ice I decided to make a joke about women's accessories. Or joke about a rap artist. The reality of the situation was that I was going to do something to make her laugh. Ezra was going to remember me.

Mom dropped me off at Israel's Pizza Parlor and I was a nervous wrecked. I bit my finger nails until they bled. My mouth was dry as sand in the desert. My shirt was soaking wet, palms sweaty, knees wobbling, and mind racing like a jet. I beat them there, so I rehearsed what I was going to say. Took a table in the back of the pizza parlor, so I could see them when they walked in. I even practiced how I was going to smile. In the middle of my rehearsal, Jericho and Ezra walked in, Jericho walking like he owned the place and Ezra strolling like a supermodel. Her long legs and sexy walk hypnotized me. She took long strides, as if she was walking in slow motion, heels making a clicking sound. Her hair bounced in unison with her clicking heels.

I waved my hand to make sure she saw me. As she moved closer, I could only imagine her being my girlfriend. I had to make her my girlfriend, but I had my doubts, too. Anyway, I was the perfect gentleman. After I gave Jericho a high-five, I stood up and pulled out her chair. "Thank you," she said.

"Welcome. My pleasure," I said. "I'm glad you guys made it," I said.

"This hungry guy wouldn't miss eating for nothing. He loves pizza, any kind of pizza," she said laughing.

"No way! I'm so hungry I could eat a horse," joked Jericho. "They have the best pizza in the world. Different types of pizza and the crust is so good. Yummy! Yummy!"

I really wasn't hungry, no appetite because I was so nervous. Food was an afterthought. I intended to seize the moment, carpe diem.

"I'm hungry, too. Let's go ahead and order," I said. "What do y'all have a taste for? I like pepperoni but I'll eat whatever."

"Pepperoni and hamburger," said Jericho.

"Nope, let's eat hamburger," said Ezra, jokingly. "Pepperoni sucks. It reminds me of hot pepper, burns your mouth!"

"That's funny because you ate the last piece of pepperoni pizza the other day," said Jericho laughing.

"Really?" I said

"Yes, really," said Jericho.

Ezra laughed lightly and said, "You know I love teasing you Jericho! Anything to get under your skin."

By this time, a tall waitress short hair stood at our table. She flipped out her green pad and asked us did we want buffet or a regular pizza. After a few seconds of thinking about it, we all decided it would be best to have buffet, especially since Jericho could eat a horse. Jericho went straight to the buffet line and Ezra excused herself to go to the bathroom. I went to the buffet line and got two plates of pizza. One for me and one for Ezra and ordered her a Pepsi. It didn't matter to me if she liked Pepsi or not. It was the thought that counted. Remember, my goal was to make her my girlfriend. First impressions meant a lot. I rushed back to the table and placed the pizza on the table, neatly place the napkins beside the plate. When she came from the bathroom, I motioned her to the table.

"Hey no need to go the buffet line, here is your pizza," I said.

"Thank you. How did you know I like Pepsi? It's my favorite soda," she said. "Did Jericho tell you Pepsi is my favorite drink?"

"Oh no, not at all. I just know what a beautiful lady likes," I said with a grin. "Besides, my Mother raised me to be nice to women."

"Yes, you're definitely nice," she said, looking surprised.

"I'm sure you are used to boys fixing your plate and taking you out to dinner," I said. She cocked her head back and gave a crazy look. I thought I said something wrong.

"Absolutely not!" she said, as her eyes widen. "Boys want one thing and one thing only. If they don't get that, then they move on. They love to play mind games and play with your heart and get you caught up in your feelings. They make you fall in love with them and then blame you when the relationship fails or if you catch them lying or cheating with another girl. It's crazy, so I've decided to stay single. Too much work."

"I see someone has had a bad experience in relationships. All boys or young men aren't the same. Some are immature and others aren't," I said, trying to sound serious.

"I beg to differ; my experiences have been rough and raw. They are all the same, carbon copy of each other," she explained. "Furthermore, I'm saving myself until marriage. The man who gets me, will be well deserving."

"Deserving of what? You can't even cook!" said Jericho laughing. "No man wants a girl who can't even boil water!"

I burst out laughing. We were so engaged in our conversation we never recognized Jericho sitting there. Ezra looked shocked when he made the comment, but nevertheless, she laughed.

"Be quite knuckle head!" she said, tapping him on his head. "I can cook better than you!"

"Oodles and noodles don't count!" said Jericho, laughing much harder. "Wait you can't even boil water!"

I laughed so hard my stomach hurt. I couldn't contain my laughter. Jericho was too funny.

"Pay him no attention!" she said laughing. "But I see you find him funny! I can cook."

"Well show me! I'll love to taste your cooking," I said.

"You'll die right there on the spot," joked Jericho.

"Whatever!" she said

"Make some spaghetti," I said. "It's my favorite dish."

"Her spaghetti tastes like soup, all watered down," joked Jericho.

"You're too funny Jericho," I said.

"He isn't funny, ole big head boy," she said laughing. Then she kissed his forehead and gave him a bear hug.

We ate our pizza and continued-laughing as Jericho continued to joke about anything and everything. I continued to engage Ezra in conversation. The conversation never got dull because I followed my script and made it all about her. When it was time to leave, I paid for the pizza, which prompted her to say, "Wow! That's a first! Hardly ever see a young man pay for a meal."

"That's what gentlemen do," I said. "You haven't met many gentlemen."

"It's not that I haven't, just not used to seeing it!" she said smiling.

"Now you can add me to that short list," I said.

"Maybe," she said, smiling.

As we walked out and I opened the door for the both of them, Jericho leaned over and whispered in her ear, while looking at me from the corner of his eye, smiling. She was smiling, too. I wonder what that meant.

"It's not nice to whisper," I joked.

"I'll tell you one day," said Jericho, laughing.

Then Jericho and I exchanged phone numbers and addresses. I dapped him up with a high-five. He told me the days he went to UNC Children's Hospital. He reminded me to come pay him a visit. I promised him I would. Ezra stared me down when I said that, but didn't say anything. I proceeded to open the car door for her.

"Thank You," she said.

"Welcome," I said. "Y'all take care and I'll see you soon Jericho."

The red and white Camaro cruised down Hillsbourgh St as the sun set and darkness fell. I could see Jericho turning around, giving me thumbs up. I didn't know what it meant at the time, but eventually I would find out. I texted Mom and told her I was ready. I sat on the bench thinking about Jericho and his beautiful sister, Ezra. I liked her already, and deep down I had a feeling she liked me, too. Maybe it was wishful thinking, but when you have cancer, wishful thinking is all you have. Because when death is the only other option, you had better make the best of it, of every good situation.

Jericho lived on a long winding road that took you through the hills and the country farms of the county. The winding round turned stepped and there sat Jericho's house at the top of the hill. The house resembled a mansion. Heck, it probably was a mansion. The huge, three-story brick house had a circular drive way surrounded by manicured bushes. Water poured out from a gigantic water fountain with three tiers. It's liked the huge water fountains you see at the mall. I parked on the side of the house near the swimming pool. That's where Mrs. Walls told me to park because Jericho wouldn't see me there. When Jericho and I exchanged numbers, he wanted me to have his mother's number, too, so that she could get to know me. I called Mrs. Walls and introduced myself and told her I would be volunteering at the UNC Hospital. I really liked Jericho; of course, I liked his sister, too. But Jericho had an effect on me that I couldn't explain. So I thought I would surprise him with a gift. I walked up the steep stairs and rang the doorbell. A small petite woman with long, black curly hair opened the door. She was gorgeous. I'm sure it was Mrs. Walls. Now I knew where Ezra had her pretty looks.

"Hello there. You must be Paul," said the woman. "I'm Mrs. Walls. It's so nice to finally meet you. You're so tall, must play basketball."

"Hello. Yes, I'm Paul Christian," I said. "So nice to meet you." I extended my right hand and with my other I gave her a vase full of flowers. "I play basketball for Enloe High School.

"Why thank you Paul!" she said excitedly. "I love flowers! Jericho is in the den playing his video games. He'll be so happy to see you."

"I hope so because I brought him a small gift. I believe he'll like this gift," I said.

"Oh trust me, he'll like it because all he does is talk about you," she said.

"Really! That's good to know," I said, shocking.

"Go down the hallway and make a left and he'll be in there," said Mrs. Walls.

"Okay," I said.

I walked slowly down the hallway, trying to surprise Jericho. I didn't want my size 18 shoes to trip me up and I fall. I would definitely be embarrassed. I got to the door of the den and peeped my head in. Jericho was playing a video basketball game. He couldn't see me. I tapped on the door lightly.

"Hey buddy! What game are you playing?" I said.

"Paul! Paul! What's up my man!" he said so excitedly. "I didn't know you were coming over! Wow what a surprise. Awesome!"

"Yes it is! But I have something I think is awesome!" I said. "Here is a gift for you. Something I believe you'll really like."

"Thanks Paul!" he said. Jericho quickly tore the wrapping off the box.

"Oh my God! Yes! 'Angels vs. Demons'! I've wanted this game for such a long time. This is the best fighting game out there! Wow! Thank You! Thank You! Thank You!" he said so happily. He jumped up and hugged me around my neck, almost causing me to lose my balance.

"Yes! Yes! Yes!" he continued to celebrate. "Now I can play online with the rest of my friends. I'll show them who is the best at this game. They'll see I'm the man. The chosen one. I have favor!"

"You're very welcome Jericho! Glad you like it," I said.

"How did you know I wanted this game?" he asked.

"Well"-I said

Before I could respond, I was interrupted.

"Mom told him," said the familiar voice.

It was Ezra, standing in the doorway with her Mother. I thought she was gone, but happy to see her.

"Yes, I told him," said Mrs. Walls. "I knew 'Angels vs. Demons' was your favorite game."

"Thanks Mom for telling Paul!" said Jericho. "Thanks again Paul for buying this game for me!"

"Now I can kick your butt in this game," joked Ezra.

"Game on!" said Jericho.

"I'll let you guys play," said Mrs. Walls.

"Oh I'm sorry Ezra; I can't play you right now. I'm going to play Paul first. I'm going to beat him in this NBA video game. Then I'll call you to whip you in 'Angels vs. Demons'!" he said laughing.

"Okay buddy," I said laughing.

"Whatever!" said Ezra, who kept staring at me.

"Go join Mom and talk about girl stuff," he joked.

Ezra shook her head and laughed, leaving Jericho and I to play the video game.

Jericho leaned back on the cushy, black recliner and explained how he was going to destroy me. He said he was undefeated playing 'NBA 2k 16'. According to Jericho, his record was a perfect 316-0. He discussed how he almost lost to guy named Goliath. Goliath was undefeated and the best online player, and sort of a bully. He told me how he destroyed him. He defeated him after having a round of chemotherapy. What at tough kid, I thought to myself.

We started the game with him scoring 10 straight points. I wanted to take it easy on him because I didn't want to embarrass him. Then he scored 10 more points. I was already down 20 points, so I decided to up the ante.

"It's on now little buddy! No more nice guy," I joked.

"Whatever! You were taking it easy on me because you think you can beat me. Nope! Not today young man," he said laughing.

"Watch this!"I said."Swish! See that 3-pointer I just hit. Opps!, there we go again. I just made another," I said. "I can play in real life and on a video game. There is no stopping me when I get young man!"

"Patience is virtue! See look how I just stole the ball from you. Going downtown…3 pointers all day long," he bragged, while drinking a Mountain Dew soda. "Are you sure you're a basketball player because you don't know how to play defense."

I shook my head in disbelief because he destroyed me. I played NBA 2k 16 all the time, but he killed me that day. I tried to play harder but he knew exactly what I was going to do before I did it.

"Man you're really good," I acknowledged. "I thought I would beat you!"

"That's what everyone says until I bring down the hammer," he said laughing.

"Well I'm no quitter," I said. "I'll fight till the end. Never give up to the enemy!"

"You're right about that. I never quit either, especially to my enemy!" he said.

"Exactly!"I said as my man dribbled the ball the court only to get his shot blocked.

"Cancer is my enemy! It's the main enemy," said Jericho, whose eyes were laser like focused on the screen. "I'll never give in to cancer. Never, I don't even think about it because that'll be giving it too much credit. I fight cancer by not acknowledging it exists, not attacking me. I see as an enemy that wants to win. Even if it kills me in the physical form, it will never kill me in the spiritual form. Never!"

There was a long pause before I said anything. Actually I had no response. How could I respond to that when cancer had ruined my life and attitude? However, I tried to see Jericho's perspective.

"Well that's good you feel that way!" I said. "I hate cancer with everything in me and I just…just…wish I could be as positive as you are."

"Always remember we have choices Paul," said Jericho, who took his eyes off the screen to give me a hard stare. "Either you're the hero or the Boogieman gets you!"

"Interesting point," I said, not knowing Ezra was standing in the doorway listening to our conversation.

"Awesome! Love your positivity Jericho," said Ezra. "Now can I play so I can kick your butt in 'Angels vs. Demons'"?

"Sure, as soon as I finish whipping Paul," said Jericho laughing.

"And he's whipping me pretty bad," I said. "This guy is a beast."

I made one last attempt to come back but I was down by 30 points with two minutes left in the game. Jericho decided to speed up the clock so the game would end quickly.

"I'll have mercy on you since I like you," said Jericho, laughing so hard he was drooling from the mouth.

"Ha ha!" I said. "Good game buddy."

"You want to play 'Angels vs. Demons'?" he asked.

"No I have a chemo appointment and I have to get back so my Mom can come with me," I said, not wanting to go because I enjoyed his company and I wanted to talk to Ezra. But I had a surprise for Ezra. I found a way to talk to her.

"So sorry you have to go," said Ezra.

"Me, too!" said Jericho, as he lowered his head like a puppy. "But I'll see you at Cancer Support Group or the UNC Hospital. You still coming to the UNC Hospital?"

"Yes I am. Trust me, I'm a man of my word," I said.

"Awesome!" said Jericho.

"That's very nice of you," said Ezra.

"I'll see you later Jericho," I said and gave him a high-five.

Mrs. Walls appeared in the door and offered me some baked cookies. I wasn't hungry but took them anyway.

"Thanks for coming by Paul. It really means a lot to Jericho and to us," she said, hugging me tightly.

"You're very welcome. Anytime you need me I'm here," I said.

"Ezra will you walk this fine gentleman out the door. He's such a blessing," said Mrs. Walls.

"Of course Mom!" said Ezra. Her beautiful smile stretched from here to New York. I smiled, too.

I had the perfect opportunity to talk to her some more. I seized this opportunity like an alligator clamping down on a gazelle. She looked gorgeous as ever. Her pink blouse and white shorts matched her white Air Jordans. Ezra ponytail made even prettier. I remained calm as we walked down the hallway and I started our conversation from the previous night.

"So are you going to cook my spaghetti? Oh that's right you can't boil water, let alone cook spaghetti!" I joked.

"I see someone has jokes! Ha! Ha!" she laughed.

"Well, I'm waiting to see!" I said.

"Keep waiting," she joked. "Besides, if I were to cook for you, you might love it and expect it all the time."

She kept laughing.

"I have all the time in the world," I said laughing. "I know how to get your attention. I know how to get you to cook me some spaghetti."

"Really? I have to hear this," she said laughing.

"Okay. But you have to close your eyes!" I said smiling.

"No way! I don't you know well enough to close my eyes!" she laughed.

"Alrighty," I said smiley. "I forgot you have to go play 'Angels vs. Demons' with Jericho. Matter of fact, he's standing on the side of the house waiting on you." I nodded in that direction and she walked towards the side of the house looking for Jericho. I quickly opened up my car door and grabbed the bouquet of flowers and a small, pink teddy bear with a white ribbon tied around it. She returned faster than I anticipated, laughing. I put the flowers and stuffed bear behind my back. My nerves were shook, sweaty palms and soaked shirt.

"You got me good!" she said laughing. "You're a prankster—"

"Surprise!, This is for you!" I said, handing her the flowers and teddy bear. She stood there with her mouth wide open! Her mouth was open I could see her tonsils.

"Thank you! Thank You! Thank You!" she said so excitedly. "I've…I've never received flowers from a boy or young man unless they expected something…never mind. This is awesome."

"Absolutely welcome. My pleasure," I said with sweat dripping from my brow. "Glad you like them, Pretty flowers for a pretty girl."

"What a sweet heart you are!" she said, still looking amazed.

My mind raced back and forth of what to say because I had to pick up Mom and go to my chemo appointment. There was a moment of silence so I said, "Let's finish this conversation over the phone because I have to go to my chemo appointment. But I'll you haven't seen the last of me Ezra."

I gave her a hug and we exchanged numbers and I jumped into my car and raced home to pick up Mom. Excitement filled my body as my heart pounded through my chest like a drum. The sweaty palms made it hard to grip the steering wheel. I rolled down the windows so that I could breathe some fresh air. I replayed the scenario of her accepting the flowers and smiling like a new born baby. She truly enjoyed receiving the flowers. I had to think of way to ask her out. I wondered if she would go out with me. I wondered would she date a teenager with cancer. That was the biggest question I wanted answered. So many questions dashed through my tiny head. Suddenly, the joy drained out of my body like a deflated balloon. My stomach tightens when I realized I still had cancer and a chemotherapy appointment to go to. Reality was a bitch, especially when you have cancer. I was happy one minute and sad the next minute. The reality of dying of cancer always loomed in my head. I gripped the steering wheel hard enough to put blisters on my hand. I bit my lip until I tasted blood. As I pulled in the driveway, I felt nauseated and weak. I grabbed my plastic bag and vomited. That was cancer. That was my reality.

Mom didn't see me vomit but I felt so weak. So I got in the passenger seat and handed Mom the keys. I all I could do was think about being nauseated. I took one of my pills and drank a coke. Mom kept cans of Coke and Sprite in the car whenever I felt sick. I laid back in the seat and fell asleep. Before I could close my eyes, Mom wanted to ask me questions.

"Hey Paul. How was your day? Was Jericho happy to see you? And did he like the game?" she asked.

"I had a nice day Mom. Jericho really enjoyed the game. We played NBA 2k 16 and he whipped me good," I said half asleep. "He's really a nice kid. Very smart and kind hearted. I really like him."

"Great Paul. I'm happy that you made a friend at the Cancer Support Group," she said, clasping her hands together. "What about his sister? Tell me about that Paul. Did you tell her how pretty she is?"

"She's beautiful Mom, prettiest girl I've even seen. She even looks better than Kitza Smith."

"Pretty girl who had your heart," teased Mom. "This young lady must be beautiful for her to look better than your Kitza Smith. You always talked about how pretty she was and how much you liked her."

"She had my heart and was pretty but she doesn't come close to young lady," I said smiling, thinking about how Ezra smiled at me when I gave her the flowers. "This young girl is beautiful Mom and I'm going to make her my girlfriend."

"What's her name?" asked Mom.

"Ezra. Ezra Walls," I said, still smiling but very nauseated. "You'll meet her one day Mom."

"I hope so Paul. A good son would let his beloved Mother see this pretty young woman," said Mom laughing. "It's clear she makes you smile. I love that. There is nothing like seeing my Paul smile."

Mom was excited for me and so was I. But I put up a front for Mom because I didn't want to stress her. Deep down I was scared of dying, didn't know if I would wake up in heaven or hell or somewhere in between for people who weren't sure about God. Ezra took my mind off about having cancer. Jericho helped me deal with the realities of cancer. Not to mention, Jericho was a special person, being around him made me happy in a different type of way.

When I arrived at the Cancer Clinic, I was very nauseated and sweating profusely. Before they called my name, I went to the bathroom to vomit some more. I felt weak but ready for the chemo so I could get it over with. Of course, they took my blood pressure and asked me how I felt. Didn't want to lie, but I told Dr. John and the gorgeous nurses, Abigail and Bathsheba, I felt okay. (By the way, they didn't look better than Ezra! Ezra put them to shame).

As I was getting my vitals checked, Dr. John asked my mother and me if I would be interested in the three week cycle. I would receive chemotherapy one week then rest for two weeks. Dr. John said the rest period would allow my body to build healthy cells. If I had healthy cells, then maybe they could scale back on the chemotherapy. That meant chemo was killing the cancer. Dr. John would ask me again after this round of chemo because if I didn't feel good, we would stick to the regular routine.

"Sounds great to me Dr. John. I hate this cancer with a passion and I'll do whatever I have to do get it out of my system," I said shaking my head back and forth. I really wanted to curse but Mom wouldn't approve of it and I would be dead wrong.

"That's the right kind of attitude to have Paul!" said Dr. John, patting me on my shoulder.

"Awesome!" said Mom, kissing me on the forehead before walking out with Dr. John

I wasn't as nervous the second time I received chemo. My vital signs were good. My heart rate was good and I didn't flinch when the nurse drew blood and when she stuck the needle into the large vein in my arm. "One week passed already," I said.

"Time flies," said Abigail. "You're more relaxed today. That is really good, which means you're getting comfortable."

"I believe I am," I said softly.

"If you need anything, let me know," she said.

"Okay," I said.

When Abigail walked out, I put on my headphones and listened to '2Pac's *Me Against the World*. I put it on repeat because it was the perfect metaphor for me: Me Against Cancer. Cancer was deadly. Cancer made me feel so lonely. It felt like I was fighting an angry Giant. A dinosaur all by myself. Because when you have cancer, it's really you against the world!

"How are you feeling Paul," asked Dr. John, while the pretty nurses Abigail and Bathsheba took notes.

"I feel sluggish and thirsty, but I'm okay," I said. Before he asked I said, "I would like to do the three week cycle. I'm ready to be healed and play basketball."

"Great. We can go ahead and set it up, and I'll write you up some more prescription. It will be stronger because you'll be getting chemotherapy more often," he said. "You're doing so good Paul. Keep the positive attitude and working hard you'll beat it. Good luck Paul."

"Thanks, Dr. John. I'm doing my best," I said softly, because I felt nauseated and weak.

"Thank you once again Dr. John," said Mom as Dr. John handed her the prescription. I told Mom I had to go to the bathroom. I vomited again and it's painful. I finished quickly so that Mom wouldn't be concerned.

On the way home, I drunk a bottle of Coke and took the big, horse pills before dozing off. I heard some soft gospel music in the background before dreaming about taking Ezra on a picnic. I surprised her with some flowers and we drove to Crabtree Lake and a nice picnic under the sun as we read poetry to each other. Only to be interrupted by Jericho wanting to go home and play 'Angels vs. Demons'. Mom interrupted my dream by gently kissing me on my forehead.

"We're home sweetie," she said in her soft southern drawl. "How are you feeling? Can I get you anything? Do you want to ~~lay~~ lie down? I can take Scooter out for a walk."

"I'm fine Mom," I said, feeling so sick I wanted to sleep for two days. "Mom would ask a thousand questions and panic if I said I didn't feel well. "I think I'll take a short nap and take Scooter for a walk. I need a nap that's all."

"You can sleep Paul and I'll take Scooter for a walk," she said. "You need rest. Alright."

"No, Mom, I'm fine. Just let me get a nap and spend time with my buddy Scooter," I pleaded with Mom. "I love my dog and he makes me feel better. And dogs are good for cancer patients."

"I guess you're right, but I don't want you walking all over Raleigh with Scooter," she joked.

"Mom you know I can't walk 20 feet without tiring out, let alone walking around Raleigh," I said. "Maybe we'll walk around NC State University."

"That'll be nice," said Mom. "Now go get some rest while I prepare your special meal."

"Okay," I said. I let myself into the house and Scooter jumped on me and licked my face. He missed me and I hadn't spent much time with him lately. "Hey buddy!" I said weakly. I was so tired I didn't have the energy to play with Scooter. Man I loved him. I could tell he was sad. I brought a ball to me and wanted to play nerf basketball, but I couldn't play. I was too weak and I ran to the bathroom to vomit again. I had never felt this bad. My stomach muscles twisted in all directions like a rope, like tug a war. Every time I heaved, my face almost went into the water. I hugged the toilet as if it were my girlfriend. After what seemed like a lifetime in the bathroom, I brushed my teeth and fell asleep. I slept the whole night and didn't wake until 11 am the next morning. I woke up because of Mom. She came in and kissed me on my forehead. Her warm kisses always woke me up. Mom cooked breakfast, but brought me fruits and vegetables instead. Apples, oranges, grapes, strawberries and fresh broccoli, and not to mention those awful tasting horse pills. I saw the greenlight on my iPhone blinking. But what next surprised me. When I looked at my text messages, there was a text from an unfamiliar number.

I clicked onto the message and it said: "Hey Paul this is Ezra. How are you doing this evening? I know you had a chemotherapy treatment and I wanted to make sure you were doing okay? I know from Jericho's chemotherapy it can be very brutal and make you tired. So I'm wishing you the best and a speedy recovery. If you need anything, let me know. Ezra."

Oh my God!!!! She texted me! She must have liked me! Wow! I thought. I couldn't believe what I just read! I reread the letter to make sure I didn't read it incorrectly. I didn't want to get too excited for the wrong thing. I reread it and it was correct. She cared about me. She cared about my well- being. Maybe I was over reacting. I needed to find out so I text her back.

Me: Hello Ezra. Thank you so much for caring about my well-being. Yes, chemotherapy can be hard and brutal and make you very tired. But I feel better than I did yesterday. Yes, I do need something. "Some of your baked spaghetti". LOL! Just joking.But if you aren't doing anything later, would you like to go to the movies? Once again, Thanks for your concerns."-- Paul

I wondered what her response would be. I fumbled my phone before turning it off. I felt like she would respond quicker if I turned off of my iPhone, superstitious. I paced up and down the stairs looking out the window, rubbing the nickels in my pockets together. My legs shaken, palms were sweaty, mouth dry as the Sierra Desert, and my stomach knotted up like a fist. I kept hesitating to turn on my iPhone. I'd tap my fingers around the turn on button before getting scared. I waited 12 minutes before I turned on my iPhone.I had a message. Was it from Ezra? I wondered.

When I turned on my phone, I had a text message from Ezra. My heart skipped a beat.

Ezra: "Hey Paul. You're very welcome. And I see you have a sense of humor about my cooking. LOL! The answer to your question is I'd love to go with you to the movies. I need to get out of the house anyway… sorry didn't mean it like it to sound like I'm using you to get out of the house. But I want to go to movies. What would you like to go see?"

I was too stunned to respond back. I jumped so high in excitement I hit my head on the ceiling. It didn't matter; I kept jumping. The nervousness had evaporated. I celebrated like I had won the NBA championship. I wasn't going to lose out on this date. But I refused to look desperate. So I waited a few more minutes before I sent my text.

Me:"That's great. There are so many movies to choose from. But I'll let you chose. Ladies first. Of course, I don't see you as using me to get out of the house…LOL…but where is baked spaghetti? LOL"

Ezra:"LOL!" No I'll rather you choose. As for baked spaghetti, well…"

Me:"Since you insist on me choosing, let's go see the movie *War Room.*"

Ezra:"Yes! I'll love to see that movie! Everyone is talking about *War Room.* I love the trailer. Looks awesome."

Me:"Cool! Will 2pm work for you?"

Ezra:"Yes it will. I'll get ready now. Which theater would you like to meet at?"

Me: "I prefer to pick you up. If you're okay with that?"

There was a long period of silence. Felt like forever before she responded.

Ezra:"Sorry for the late response, but I was on the phone with my

Mother. Yes, you can come pick me up. That's fine. I told my Mother, she thinks it's a great idea."

Me: "That'll work for me. Do you have enough time to get ready because I know how slow women are. LOL"

Ezra: "LOL! Whatever! I'll see you soon."

Me: "LOL! Alright!"

I screamed so loud that Scooter hid underneath the bed. Mom burst through the door like a fireman.

"Paul baby what's wrong? Are you okay!! Oh My God!" yelled Mom.

"I'm fine Mom. I'm going on a date with Ezra!" I said jumping up and down on my bed. "We're going to the movies Mom! Going to the movies!"

"Fantastic Paul!" said Mom standing with her hands on her hips. "You don't have to scare me like that. I thought something was really wrong. My goodness Paul. You almost gave me a heart attack! Just happy you're okay."

"Sorry Mom. I can't. Can't...explain how I'm feeling right now! She's beauty queen! Like USA beauty queen," I said, tired and queasy after all of the jumping.

"What movie are you going to see?" asked Mom, who was relieved.

"War Room," I said.

"You'll love that movie," she said with a smile on her face, as she left the room.

"Amazing! Everyone says it's a really good movie," I said happily.

I laid out my nicest clothes and most popular sneakers. I cleaned my retro Jordans, the red and black kind. Those were the most popular sneakers. After I showered and brushed my teeth, I sprayed myself with some Boss Cologne. Not only was I going to smell good, I was going to look good, too. I swallowed the big horse pills to prevent any vomiting. I had to make a lasting impression. This was a date, after all. But it was my opportunity to win her over. To show her there was more to me than having cancer.

I wanted to get there early, so that I could talk to Mrs. Walls and play a few video games with Jericho. I took the highway to get there faster and rehearsed my script. Yeah, I wrote a script because I wanted a smooth interaction. I was one thing to joke with her in the presence of Jericho or in her own home. But it would be totally different on a date. We would get to talk about different things that teenagers talk about.

Since I took the highway, I arrived at her house, the mini mansion, in about 15 minutes. I swished a small amount of Listerine in my mouth before I got out of the car. I knocked on the door and Ezra answered the door wearing a baby blue shirt with white blue jeans and retro Carolina blue Air Jordans. She wore her silky, black hair down to her back. Her white teeth glistened with sparkle in her hazel green eyes. Ezra looked more like a model for Cover Girl magazine than a pretty young lady going out on a date. She was beyond sexy And beyond beautiful. I was lucky.

"Hey Paul," she said smiling.

"Hello Ezra. You look beautiful," I said, as I gave her a warm hug. "These are for you." I gave her a bouquet of roses. Once again, she was surprised.

"Thank You Paul! Thank You!" she said smiling, "You're full of surprises. You're such a gentleman. Wow! Let me put these pretty flowers in a vase. I'll be right back."

"Welcome! Very welcome!" I said. "Glad I can make you smile." I took the opportunity to talk to Jericho, who was sitting at the table eating some carrots. He was wearing a red and black scarf, a Wolfpack jersey with matching wrist bands.

"Hey there Jericho," I said, giving him a high-five. "How is it going buddy."

"What's going on man!" he said, jumping up to give me a high-five. "I'm good man. Feeling better and ready to play some real basketball. Have you been practicing since that I whipped you the last time?"

"Of course," I said laughing, "you got lucky little buddy! I'll beat you the next time."

"Ha-Ha-Ha!" he said laughing. "You're expertise needs attention, you're very challenged in playing NBA 2k 16! But I'll help you."

I laughed so hard my stomach hurt. "Whatever buddy," I said. "I'll beat you next time."

"Let's go now!" he said, slapping me on my arm. "This game isn't for the weak and weary! You got time to take a quick butt whipping."

"Okay! Let's go buddy! It's on!" I said laughing. "You going to regret you played me!"

"Talk is cheap!" he said.

"We'll see!" I said.

Jericho pressed the power button on the PlayStation 4 and sat right beside me on the black leather coach. He was a trash talker to the 10th degree. Sitting this close to him, I finally saw the red marks on the back of his neck, along with a scar underneath his arm. I knew it came from cancer.

"Ready?" he said excitedly. "I'll make it quick. The first one to 12 wins."

"Oh yeah," I said, still thinking about the marks on his body.

The basketball game started and his man won the tip off. He dribbled up the court, crossed over my man, stepped back and hit a 3 pointer.

"See that deadly move Paul?" said Jericho laughing. "It's only going to get better. But worse for you."

"That was luck," I said laughing. "Watch this."

I steered my man to midcourt and did a crossover, behind the back move and shot a 3 pointer. Then I had my man steal the inbounds pass score a quick lay-up. On the next play, I trapped him and stole the ball, passed it the open man and hit another 3-pointer. Score 8-3.

"Hey man what has gotten into you," said Jericho, laughing and surprised at the same time. "Have you been practicing?"

"Doesn't matter. Take this whipping like a man!" I joked.

"Okay, no more Mr. Nice guy. You're going down like the titanic. Watch this," said Jericho. "My man is crossing you up now, drop step, pivot, jump shot, and swish!"

"Lucky shot!" I said, pressing my button faster so my man could dribble up the court. "My man is going behind his back and deadly crossover bam! Slam dunking baby!"

"Oh that's nothing," said Jericho. "You can't guard me; look at that crossover, behind back quick pass to my other guy, WHAM! 3-pointer! Game tied BABY!"

I laughed at Jericho mocking me. I looked at my watch and realized the movie started in about 40 minutes but I wanted to beat Jericho, too. Ezra hadn't come to get me yet so I had time to finish him off.

"Stop looking at your watch! I'm going to finish you off so you can go to the movies," said Jericho with a smile on his face. "I leave no prisoners!"

"I'm about to finish you off," I said. "Bam! See that 3 pointer!"

"Crossover, slam dunk!" he shouted. "I just stole the ball, another 3 pointer! Game over!"

"Lucky shot man!" I said, laughing at my buddy. "I'll get you the next time."

"I need a practice player!" laughed Jericho.

"Whatever!" I laughed.

"Did you guys have fun?" said Ezra, who had entered the room with that pretty smile.

"Yeah, he beat me again! I said, shaking my head and smiling at the same time. "I'll beat the next time."

"In your dreams," laughed Jericho.

I laughed."Your luck will run out!" I said. "I'll see you soon," I said to Jericho as we exchanged high-fives.

"And you better take care of my sister. Or there will be consequences!" joked Jericho.

"Okay buddy!" I laughed. "I don't want to hear about any of your consequences."

"He's too funny," said Ezra.

Before we walked out of the house, Mrs. Walls said, "Have fun guys! And don't spend all of Paul's money and eat too much!"

"Mom!!" laughed Ezra. "I don't eat a lot."

"Too funny! Didn't know you were a big eater," I said, laughing at her while admiring her beauty, and thinking of a conversation to the way to the movies.

"See you later Mom. I'll be home after the movies," said Ezra.

"Nice seeing you again Mrs. Walls," I said.

"Likewise," said Mrs. Walls.

We walked out of the mini mansion and I politely opened up the door for her. She smiled so elegantly, like a Queen hold court. I was nervous, but it was a good nervous. Butterflies were flying in my stomach like a jet. Once again, I was going to win her over. I stayed on script, but the script wasn't making sense. I had to think of something fast to talk about on the ride to the movies because we definitely couldn't talk during the movie. Suddenly, I recognized a Carolina Tar Heels ring on her pinky finger. Now I had something to talk about. Because I hated the UNC Tar Heels with a passion. I was a die-hard Wolfpack fan! And we hated the Tar Heels.

"Why are you wearing that ugly ring on your pinky finger?" I asked her joking.

"Huh?" she said looking surprised at my response. "Oh that's me representing my Tar Heels! Tar Heels Nation! That's my team. The best team in the nation. Number 1 every year!"

"Whatever! I Hate the Tar Heels! My goodness, how can a young lady so pretty stoop so low to like UNC-CHEAT! Well I guess there is something wrong with everyone! Even the pretty ones!" I joked, waiting for her response.

"I know you're not talking about my Heels! No we don't cheat," she said laughing so hard she had to catch her breath. "Look, as far as I'm concerned, they're not the cheaters. That was the women's basketball team. Not the men's basketball team. We do things the Carolina way!"

"Yep! You sure do! Fake classes, players not doing their work, a phantom assignment, that's the Carolina way! Nothing like cheating your way to victories!" I said laughing.

She kept laughing. She was stomped; I got her.

"Once again, that was mainly the women's basketball team," she said, continuing to laugh. Her laugh was so sweet and innocent. "So who do you like Mr. Paul? Because you have so much to say about my Mighty Tar Heels! Let me guess, you probably like those stinking Duke Blue Devils!"

"What are you crazy woman!" I said jokingly, "I'm a Wolfpack fan, all day and every day. Best basketball team around. We win baby and we don't cheat. Our players actually go to class! But you and UNC CHEAT don't understand the meaning of class work, let alone academics."

"The Wolfpack? Are you kidding me! The Wolfpack haven't won a championship since 1983! 1983!" she said, laughing so hard she was holding her stomach. "My Mother was in the fourth grade the last time they won a basketball championship! God knows that was like a thousand years ago! I believe the last time the Wolfpack won a championship was in the 20th century!"

I laughed harder and harder the more she talked. That was a good one. I didn't have a good come back, but I had accomplished my goal by generating a good conversation filled with laughter.

"Alright that's true, but can you explain why former basketball star Rashad McCants blew the whistle on your Almighty Tar Heels? I asked with a big grin on my face."

She looked at me and stuck out her tongue.

"He's a traitor and he's mad!" she said laughing. "He's upset for whatever reason. He's a hater! And so are you!"

I kept laughing because we both were right about our respective basketball programs. She was dead right about the Wolfpack not winning a championship since 1983 and I was right about the cheating scandal. The conversation was flowing. I had her attention. Then I said, "You're still cheaters!"

"Whatever!" she said smiling.

"We'll see,who's the better team this season," I said.

At this point, I pulled into the Brier Creek Theater and told Ezra to wait while I opened her car door. She stepped out of the car like Ms. America, long legs, pretty smile, and hair flowing, the only thing missing was her waving at the crowd. Speaking of a crowd, the movie theater was packed that day. The line stretched into the adjacent parking lot. The tickets were free courtesy of me having cancer. I would receive many benefits because of having cancer. It amazed me that a person has to have a disease or be dying to get free stuff. I told the lady at the window my name and she told Ezra and me to follow her. I recognized several people at the movie theater. And so many people knew Ezra, too. I felt the paparazzi were following us.

"Hey Paul," said a girl named Mya from school, who was with a group of girls. "How are you?"

"I'm fine, doing okay. Hope you're doing fine," I said and kept walking because I didn't have time to talk.

"Paul! What's up dude," said another boy from school.

"Paul!" said someone I didn't know.

Then everyone spoke to Ezra. It was like walking with a famous person.

"Ezra Walls! Hey, there," said one girl wearing an outfit suited for Halloween.

"Hello Ezra," said a group of girls ordering snacks.

"Hey there," said Ezra.

"Hey Ezra," said a two teenage boys who were tall like me. "Nice to see you," said one of the boys.

"Nice to see you all too," said Ezra.

"Everyone knows you. You're a Superstar!" I said laughing.

"Far from it," she said laughing. "I just know a lot of people. That's all."

The lady took us to a suite that sat in a corner above the theater. The suite looked like a small apartment with a long, red circular couch, a two love seats with cup holders, a mahogany table that seated six, a two huge flat screen televisions with remote controls, an automated popcorn machine, a refrigerator full of different types of juices, sodas, fruits, vegetables, a small kitchen with a huge microwave, a bathroom with decorative towels, and big bowl of candy bars, mainly nutritious. To top it off, we could watch any of the movies at the theater.

"Wow! This is amazing. I mean…amazing," I said with my mouth wide open.

"Absolutely awesome," said Ezra, whose eyes were so wide it looked like they would pop out of her head. "I'm speechless."

"This is yours for the entire duration!" said the lady, who was very nice. "If you need anything, just push the intercom button and I'll be here. Enjoy yourselves and my name is Mary."

"Thank you so much Ms. Mary!" said Ezra and I at the same time.

"Can you believe this place!" said Ezra. "This is unbelievable."

"Yes, this is something special," I said. I knew I had to seize the moment, continue to have a great time. My nerves were shook. Sweat poured underneath my shirt. I took a deep breath and remained calm. So I told Ezra to relax and asked her what would she like to eat and drink.

"Something fruity to drink and a big box of popcorn will be fine," she said smiling.

"Alrighty," I said smiling. "Don't be afraid to eat up everything, either."

"I see you got jokes," she laughed. "I don't eat a lot. Just candy. I have a sweet tooth."

I laughed at her. The thought of having her as my girlfriend made me not think about cancer. I felt free with her, almost like a fairy tale with a happy ending. It reminded me of the story of Beauty and the Beast. She was the beauty. And I was the beast. The beast being cancer.

I grabbed the scooper and packed her box full of popcorn and brought back some skittles and a Welch's' fruit punch. I put all of it in a container and brought it to her. I took my seat beside her and turned off the lights and watched the previews before the movie started. All I could think about was spending more time with her.

End of Chapter

When the movie started, I made a decision not to talk, only if I had to ask her a question. I hated when people talked during a movie. And I didn't want to be known as the person who talked during a movie.The movie *War Room* surprised us on so many levels, emotionally, spiritually, and ethically. The movie was about a married couple struggling to keep their marriage afloat. Elizabeth was a successful real estate agent and her husband Tony was a successful businessman, lived in an affluent neighborhood, and had a beautiful daughter. Because Tony treated Elizabeth awful, she became bitter and their marriage suffered. Elizabeth was about to give up on her marriage until she met her new client, Miss Clara. Miss Clara told Elizabeth to pray for her husband and their marriage through scripture. Miss Clara introduced her to a wall full of scriptures about praying for her own husband, known as the *War Room*.

"This movie is very interesting," said Ezra, tears flowing down her cheeks as she watched an emotional with the daughter. "The little girl knows her parents' marriage is failing. Poor girl."

It was an emotional scene, so I handed her some Kleenex and put arms around her. She kept crying. "I know it's difficult. She'll be okay, eventually," I whispered into her ear.

"I hope so. Kids shouldn't have to suffer because of selfish parents. Or because of her self-centered father," she said.

"I agree," I said, thinking about how Dad died of cancer, still upset he wasn't here. Deep down I felt like Dad didn't do enough to fight cancer. I stopped thinking about it because I became frustrated.

Ezra clapped loudly when Elizabeth forgave Tony for his transgressions, for having a mistress and disrespecting her. Tony lost his job for doing something illegal, and Elizabeth stayed with him because she loved Jesus. Elizabeth believed marriage was 'til death do us part.'

The movie ended and we discussed the movie like movie critics. Actually, Ezra was the movie critic.

"What a powerful woman to stand by her man during her difficult marriage," said Ezra. "The power of prayer". Prayer works. Prayer is awesome. You can accomplish anything with prayer. No matter how tall the obstacle, you can overcome it with prayer. Never underestimate the power of prayer."

When she made the statement, she looked directly at me, as if to say I need prayer. Or that I could pray cancer. I had no response. I shook my head up and down, like I agreed with her.

"Oh yeah! Oh yeah! I guess prayer worked for Elizabeth," I said, not knowing what she meant by the power of prayer. I'd heard Mom talk about the power of prayer, but I wasn't sold on it, not yet anyway. Mom was a Christian, believed in prayer and stuff, but for some reason it went over my head. For instance, if God was so great, why did He let people get diseases and die? Whatever the reason, I wanted Ezra to downplay it as much as possible.

"It certainly did work for her," said Ezra, referring to the power of prayer that helped save Elizabeth's marriage. "Prayer works if you believe in it. If you believe in God. I know everyone doesn't believe in God and I don't try to force my beliefs on people, but when people get sick or there is a natural disaster, the first thing they do is ask for prayer!"

"Very interesting," I said, thinking of a way to change the conversation. I wanted to make a smooth transition from prayer to something humorous. "Well, prayer is something your Tar Heels are going to need with this cheating scandal."

"Oh man! Here you go again with that mess," said Ezra, laughing. "We don't need prayer; your sorry Wolfpack needs prayer."

"We don't cheat," I joked. I took the opportunity to get her another

Welch's juice. "Here you go. I see how much you like Welch's fruit punch."

"Thank you so much!" she said. "You're so sweet. What a gentleman."

"You're well deserving," I said."Is there anything else you want? Popcorn, candy, money!" She laughed and shook her head. Then flashed her gorgeous smile. I kept reminding myself to seize the moment, to take advantage of the opportunity. I planned for us to go the lake afterwards. That was my grand surprise for her.

"Hey what time do you have to be home," I asked.

"I don't really have a curfew," said Ezra. "But I try not to come home too late; don't want to disrespect Mom or anything."

"Alright, that's cool," I said, grinning like a kid at Christmas.

"Why what's up? Asked Ezra curiously. She flashed that ~~smile~~ gorgeous smile again, making me melt. "Hello!"

"I want to take you somewhere," I said.

"Where?" she asked.

"It's a surprise," I said.

"Surprise! Mmmmm…don't know about that. You might be a kidnapper," she said jokingly. "Let me text my mother and tell her you're taking me somewhere to surprise me."

"Come on now!" I said laughing. "I've never known someone with cancer to be a kidnapper." She laughed really hard. She was enjoying herself.

"Let's go. I like surprises," she said smiling.

"Cool, let's go," I said.

I opened up the door for Ezra and thanked Ms. Mary for the free movie and great hospitality. Instead of going through the regular movie crowd, Ms. Mary led us to out of a side door to the parking lot.Ms. Mary gave me a free movie pass for a year and a basket full of all types of goodies. I would have access to the movie suite, too. That was amazing.

"Thank you so much Ms. Mary," I said.

"Welcome. Enjoy and God Bless you on this journey. I'll keep you my prayers for you to make a full recovery," said Ms. Mary.

"I appreciate your prayers," I said.

"Thank you so much and thank you for praying for him," said Ezra, which surprised me.

I walked Ezra to my car and opened the door for her. As we drove away, I saw everyone waving at her. It was clear Ezra was a popular young lady. I wanted to know how many guys she had dated or basically why she was single. Before I could ask that question, she asked me a question.

"What are your thoughts about the movie? How do you feel about the power of prayer?" she asked.

I cleared my throat and tried to give a decent answer. But I wanted to be honest, too. "I liked the movie. It showed that marriage is difficult, but it can be salvaged if you believed in the institution of marriage and the power of prayer," I said, still not understanding what I had just said. "But a person has to believe in God first and foremost to believe in the power of prayer. Quite frankly, I don't know if I believe in the power prayer."

She was a long silence. She turned her head and looked out of the window. I wondered had I made her mad. Why was there a pause? *I messed up now, I thought.* I had to speak my mind. What was I thinking? There were a hundred thoughts going through my mind. It seemed forever before she said anything.

"Do you mind me asking why you don't believe in the power of prayer?" she asked, staring at me like a reporter looking for a good sound bite.

"I just don't for obvious reasons. For there to be a God and for people to die, I don't understand what prayers do," I said, trying to look at her from the corner of my so I could see her face. Since I was driving, I couldn't see her face. I had no idea what her facial expressions looked like.

"Okay. I understand that reason. I've heard people say that, too. It's amazing where some people believe in God and prayer and some don't. I guess it just depends...," she said, smiling. "I guess it's how you're raised, too. If you go to church regularly and that's all your parents preach, then you start to believe in it. But you believe in it once you see that it really works."

"Yeah, I can understand that," I said, raising my eyebrows, not knowing how to respond to her statement. There was an awkward silence and I didn't know how to change the subject. I stayed on the subject matter, thinking it would naturally lead to another conversation.

"My mother believes in the power of prayer. When my father was dying with cancer, she prayed day and night, staying by his side. She read biblical scriptures to him every day. They prayed together. She prayed with my father up until the day he died. She did all of that praying for him and with him and he still died," I said softly, not realizing how devastated I was about Dad's death. "So I just don't understand how people pray to God asking Him to heal a love one and they still die. Then others pray and God answer their prayers and their love ones live. It's like God picked and chooses. I don't understand. I don't believe I'll ever understand. Maybe it's not for me to understand."

"I'm so sorry you lost your father. I'm really sorry you lost your father. My heart goes out to you," said Ezra. "I...I...didn't mean to make you sad or anything," she said with remorse. "I can understand why you don't believe in prayer...I'm so sorry."

"Oh no you're fine. It's okay," I told her, reassuring her by placing my hand on hers. "I've been struggling with that forever, ever since he died. He's been dead about eight months, I guess. I try not to think about it."

"Oh my God! How could I be so selfish and bring up a subject about the power of prayer and God and your father is deceased, she said, beating herself up for no apparent reason. "Forgive me I'm so sorry."

"No, no, it's fine Ezra. Trust me it's okay," I said, reassuring her by patting her soft hands. "You're not being selfish because you didn't know my father was dead. Besides, it's about time I talk about my father."

"I know, but I just feel bad about it, that's all," she said."Especially with cancer and all, knowing that Jericho has it."

"It's alright Ezra. It's not a problem," I reassured her. "I have something to make you feel better." By now, we had arrived at Lake Crabtree and I got out of the car and opened up my trunk. I had bouquet roses, a small white teddy bear, and a box of candy. I brought along some Welch's fruit punch from the movie theater. Put it in a decorated box. I peeped through the back window to make sure she wasn't looking at me. I closed the trunk and walked slowly towards the passenger side. My heart raced faster and faster as I approached her side of the car. She was texting, so I took a deep breath before I opened up her door. I grabbed her hand and asked her to follow me. We walked down the long path towards the lake, past the park, and picnic tables. Sweat poured down my chest and I twirled the ring on my finger. She was smiling, but silent.

"Where are we going?" she asked.

"It's a surprise," I said.

"Okay," she said smiling.

"We're almost there," I said. My breathed gets deeper and deeper, trying to conceal it from her. I stayed nervous whenever we were together. We were getting closer. My heart raced faster.

As we got closer to the lake, I asked her to turn around for a few minutes. I promised her wasn't going to do anything to her. I pulled the box out and told her to turn around. I handed her the box and she flashed that gorgeous smile. She slowly opened the box and flashed and said, "Oh my thank you! This is so sweet. I love these roses and the teddy bear. It's so cute. You're just a sweetheart. I've never met a guy so sweet as you!" she said, giving me a long, tight hug. "You're full of surprises Paul! I never know what you're going to do."

"You're very welcome. I love surprising you," I said. "A wonderful young lady like you deserves to be surprised. But I'm not done yet."

"What? There's more?" she asked.

"Of course!" I said laughing. I grabbed her hand and we walked over to the pier where an older man wearing a white baseball cap was waiting with a midsize blue and white yacht. The number 316 was inscribed on the side in black letters. I told the man who I was and gave him my ticket.

"Good afternoon young man and young lady," said the man, whose name was Mr. Timothy.

"Hello Mr. Timothy," I said. "This is an awesome yacht."

"Hello there Mr. Timothy," said Ezra. "I agree, this yacht is awesome."

"Thank you. Thanks a lot. I'm going to ride y'all around on the lake today, let y'all experience nature's beauty. Enjoy the ride," he said in his southern drawl. "This is a tour you'll never forget."

"Can't wait!"said Ezra.

"Very nice. This will be exciting," I said. "That's what I was hoping for." I helped Ezra onto the yacht and led her to the front of the yacht. I wanted us to have the best view as we sailed around Lake Crabtree. But I changed my mind and we walked up the mini-stairs, where I surprised her with a long rose and a box of chocolate. A Pretty pink teddy bear sat on top of the box. Ezra eyes widen, mouth opened. She smiled and put her hands over her mouth.

"Oh my God! You're amazing Paul! All of this for me!" she said excitedly. "I don't understand why you're doing this. But I absolutely love it. This is amazing! This reminds me of what my father used to do for my Mom! Thank you again Paul! You are by far the best!"

"You are so welcome. I want you to have a good time, to enjoy yourself," I said.

"I am!" she said. "The flowers, the teddy bear and the chocolate". You know exactly what I like. I...I...I don't get treated like this. I'm not use to this."

"Well, get used to it because I'm full of surprises," I said laughing. "I always have a trick up my sleeve."

"Yeah I bet you do have a trick up your sleeve," she said jokingly. "I'm sure you do this with all of the girls you meet! I bet you're a pro at doing this!"

"No way!" I laughed.

"Yeah, whatever, tell me anything!" she said, continuing to laugh.

I could only laugh, too. The fact that a pretty young lady like her was sitting with me on a yacht blew my mind. I never saw this happening. Honestly, I was surprised she would go out on a date with a teenager suffering from cancer. Maybe she felt sorry for me. Maybe she felt obligated because I had befriended her baby brother, Jericho. Honestly, there was a reason, a deeper reason. My gut told me that. I tried to figure out the reason, but I would find out sooner than later.

Mr. Timothy asked us were we ready to cruise around the lake. We both yelled out yeah. I believe he was more excited than we were. But we were very excited, too. She kept smiling and shaking her head at the surprise. I'm sure she wanted to know why we were sailing around a lake in a mid-size yacht. She never asked. Basically, it was Mom's idea. Mom and I were supposed to ride on the yacht and spread Dad's ashes across Lake Crabtree. It was Dad's favorite place. He fished there, ran through the jogging trail, and that's where he proposed to Mom. He spent so much time there with Mom; it was like their second home. She was his first and only love. They had so many fond memories, but we spent so much time there together as a family. That made it very special to Dad. That's where he taught me how to fish. And he wanted us to spread his ashes over Lake Crabtree seven months from the day he died. The number seven was his favorite number. Most importantly, Mom wanted me to enjoy myself with Ezra. She believed Ezra and I could enjoy the yacht like her and Dad used to do. Mom felt like I would be with Dad in spirit. We decided we would come back to the lake later in the evening and spread his ashes. I loved Mom because she wanted me happy. The lengths a mother would go to help her cancer ridden son.

Mr. Timothy set the yacht in motion and said, "Let's enjoy this beautiful day!" Ezra and I stared at the amazing beauty of the lake and the rolling hills that surrounding it. The sun shined brightly on our faces. The kids played and swam in a roped off area. It was hundreds of yards away from the where the yachts sailed. And my confidence soared whenever I looked at Ezra. She kept staring at me while she ate her chocolate. Once again, I reminded myself I had to make my time with her count, although it seemed like she was having an awesome time. I had to know for sure. I wasn't about to get fooled again, thinking a female likes me and she wants to only be friends. The friend zone was awful. Under no circumstances was I going to be in the friend zone.

"So how are you feeling right now?" I asked. "I see you like the chocolate."

"I'm enjoying myself and the beauty of Lake Crabtree. This is such a beautiful place. Yes, the chocolate is scrumptious," she said, stuffing more chocolate into her mouth. "I've never been treated like this before. I'm still in shock that a young man like you would treat me so nice and special without wanting something in return. Never met a guy like you before. I swear I haven't."

"Really? I find that hard to believe," I said jokingly. "You're too pretty to not have been treated like a queen. Come on now, this is the norm for you."

"Yeah right!" she laughed out loudly. "You just don't know how boys are or young men for that matter. It's always a hidden agenda. They're nice and sweet in the beginning and will do anything for you or buy you stuff, but then they expect sex in return. I'm not the one for that, no sir. I'm no prostitute."

"Okay! A girl with standards!" I said laughing. "A pretty girl with standards at that!"

"Absolutely!" she said.

"Awesome!" I said.

"That's how I was raised. That's how my parents raised me, especially my Daddy! My Daddy told me how boys operated and the lies they would tell to sleep with a girl. He prepared me well!"

"A Daddy's girl!" I said smiling.

"Exactly!" she said laughing. "My Daddy knew best!"

"Yeah they do," I said, looking at the beautiful water splashing on the boat and thinking about my own Dad. I changed the subject because I didn't want to think about Dad, not now anyway. Well, she changed the subject.

"Alright, so what's your story?" she asked.

"What story?" I asked back.0

Ezra cocked her back and looked at me sideways, as if I knew what she was talking about. Then she curled up her lips and flashed a sarcastic smile. I had no idea what she meant. "What story?" I asked again, smiling.

"Don't play dumb Mr. Paul. You know what story I'm talking about," she said laughing historically. "Everyone has a story, especially young boys."

I threw my hands up in the air because I was clueless. Girls loved to fish for details and get guys to talk and find out information. Still, I was lost in the conversation. "What in the world are you talking about?" I asked again, still laughing at her.

"Okay, since you want to play games I'll tell you," she said smiling. "Why are you single? A tall and popular basketball player who is handsome doesn't go unnoticed. Of course, you probably have your pick of the litter. Hey, what does a girl like me know?"

She grinned and gave me a sarcastic look. She acted as if she knew something about me or the girls at my school. I believed she knew a lot about me. But I played it cool. The conversation was interesting. But

I was going to keep her guessing or at least find out who she knew. I understood what she meant. I wanted her to keep probing so we could talk forever.

"Ha! Ha!" I said with mock laughter. "I want to thank you for the compliments and I have to wonder who you know at my school. Because you're dead set that I'm supposed to have a girlfriend or have all of these girls wanting me. Or that I can get pick any girl that I wanted…. whatever." Ezra laughed and shook her head. Then she smiled and looked at me with amazement.

"Mr. Paul I love how you play so innocent," she said laughing. "No need to play innocent with me. Because I know the truth. Good looking young men don't walk around single. For all I know you might be a serial player."

She leaned her head back and laughed out loud. We both laughed. She had the funniest laugh, a mixture of southern drawl and a cartoon character. Her laughter was hilarious. It calmed my nerves tremendously. We were engaged in a good conversation that could last for hours. That's what I wanted, a conversation that could carry over to the night. I liked the fact that she thought I was handsome. My confidence kept growing. So I grabbed her hand and walked her over to end of the yacht, where the view was beautiful. I looked into her eyes and said, "it doesn't matter why I'm single and if I can get any girl I want. What matters is that I wanted to spend this day with you. I wanted to enjoy this day with you! You and you only! All the other stuff I don't care about. I wouldn't spend time like this with just any female. This day is special to me and I wanted to spend it with someone who I believe is special in her on way. So let's enjoy this moment, cherish it."

I hugged her and kissed her forehead. She laid her head close to my chest and hugged me back harder. Ezra remained silent as she just hugged me. It amazed me she kept hugging me and not letting me go. I waited for a response, but heard only silence. I wondered if she was okay. She squeezed me tighter, sucking the air out of my stomach. The silence stiffened. I rubbed my fingers through her hair, hoping to spark her to talk. But nothing happened. She kept holding me tighter, as if she didn't want me to go. I started to worry.

"Are you okay," I whispered in her ear. "You're very quiet."

"Yeah I'm fine. I had a flashback. A memory of so long ago," she said softly.

"What memory is that?" I asked.

"A memory of me and my Dad, when I was a little girl!" she said.

"What was the memory about?" I asked "Or is it a private memory."

"It's not private at all. My Dad used to take me and Jericho to Atlantic Beach and he always made me feel special. He always said I was his baby, his first love," she said slowly, smiling at the thought as you looked me in the eyes. "This reminds me of how we would all go fishing as a family, but Dad made it a point to make sure I received his attention and love. Dad always told me that if a young man didn't treat me with respect, genuineness, and some attention, he wasn't for me. He told me to always seek those traits in a guy. The guy must make me feel special like my Dad made me feel. And you make me feel very special Paul. Just like my Daddy! That means a lot to me!"

I was stunned. Speechless! Surprised! And excited! I remained calmed, though.

"Wow! Very interesting. I feel so privileged to remind you of your father," I said, hugging her tighter. If you think that much of your father, this is truly an honor. I'll definitely treat you with respect, genuineness and a lot of attention. You're very special."

"No Paul, you're very special! You don't act like other guys!" she said softly. You could be doing so many other things, especially with your condition. But you are friends with Jericho. You spend time with him, and you truly like him. That means so much to me and my Mother. When someone can do something that's bigger than themselves, and not expect anything in return, it means they are selfless and have a purpose in life."

I stood there in silence and stared at her. I wanted to kiss her because that's what people do in situations like that. Or that's what I saw in the movies. I was afraid to kiss her because she might move her face. So I caressed her hair, kissed her forehead and placed her head in my chest.I would kiss her another time, I thought to myself. I held her hand and we sat down as the yacht continued to cruise. A song called "Halo" by Beyoncé played blasted through the loud speakers. What a coincidence I thought to myself.

"Thank you so much Ezra!" I said still holding her hand. "For you to see me in a positive light really means a lot to me. But to compare me to your Dad is extra special. Those are some big shoes to fill...man...I'm really in the twilight zone right now. Everything is happening so fast I can't even blink my eyes. And Jericho is the one very special person I might add. He's very positive. I've learned so much from him in such a very short time."

"Yes he's very positive. I love Jericho so much! He's my heart! That's my baby! He looks so much like our Daddy!" she said smiling, looking up at the sky. "He would be so proud of him and how he's fighting. He's a fighter like Dad!"

Ezra talked as if her father was deceased. I wasn't sure. No way was I about to ask. I figured she would tell me.

"I'm sure he is. He's a fighter for sure," I said.

"Dad was a fighter until the day he died! He died from that ugly disease we call cancer, pancreatic cancer to be exact!" she said sadly, but with a slight smile on his face. "Dad suffered from cancer. He lost weight, his hair, and his ability to do the things he loved, like fishing and spending time with us. But cancer couldn't take away his smile, his laughter and his spirit. There is nothing worse than seeing someone die from cancer. It has to be the worse way to die. To see Dad finally transition to heaven was glorious for me. God took him away from his misery and suffering. I wasn't going to be that selfish daughter who wanted their father to live only for their satisfaction, but at the cost of him suffering and dying miserably. I wasn't going to be that child."

Of course, I was speechless. Ezra made so much sense when she talked. She was one of those people that when she talked, you responded with intelligence, no nonsense. I wanted to say something profound and sound super intelligent. I decided not to.

"So sorry for your loss! So sorry to hear about your Dad dying. Oh man, I know that was painful. I feel your pain. I know how you felt," I said, shaking my head and thinking about my own father. Then I placed my arm around her shoulder and said, "it's going to be alright."

"Thank you!" she said softly, embracing me.

"Welcome!" I said. I continued to hold her as we both listened the lyrics of the song "Halo". We started singing the song softly. The song was on repeat because it kept playing, which was strange because neither one us requested the song. That was either a conscience or fate. I wondered was I Ezra's *halo*, or was she mine. Because the song was about finding someone who was your halo or angel! I felt lost in translation. Things were happening too fast and I felt nauseated. Somehow I dealt with. But as the sun settled and dawn fell upon us, Ezra asked me if I wanted to slow dance. So we slow danced as it became dark and night grew silent. We slow danced to *Halo* and Ezra laid her head in my chest. I knew how to slow dance by watching Dad and Mom dance in the living room. I was too excited to concentrate because it seemed unreal. Everything seemed unreal, having cancer and dancing with the prettiest girl I'd ever seen. But for the first time in a long time, I had something to smile about.

End Chapter

When the yacht ride ended, Mr. Timothy asked us did we enjoy ourselves and we were welcome to come anytime. We both thanked him for such a great time. Before we left, Mr. Timothy whispered in my ear and said, "God didn't give us the spirit of fear." Then he handed me a small piece of paper with a bunch of mixed up words that he said I should unscramble. He said once I unscrambled the words, I would understand what he meant. I told him I would. I hurried up to the car because I wanted to get Ezra home at a decent hour, even if she didn't have a curfew.

I opened up Ezra's car door and jumped into the driver's seat quickly. Not only did I want to get home, but I wasn't feeling well. My stomach hurt and I felt nauseous. On the ride home, Ezra talked excessively. I had no problem with her talking because I didn't feel well and I enjoyed hearing her talk, especially about how she enjoyed herself.

"I know I've I told you before how special you are, but it really means a lot to me in how you went out of your way to show me a great time," she said. "I appreciate that!"

"You're very welcome!" I said through clenched teeth. My stomach was hurting and I felt sick. I drove faster so I could get her home. It took forever because every stoplight was red. Whenever a person was in a hurry, it seemed as if everything got into the way. But I wasn't about to be quiet because I didn't want to seem rude.

"Maybe we can do this another time, if you aren't too busy!" I joked, waiting for her to say something smart. "We can definitely talk about your cheating Tar Heels!"

"Ha!Ha! Real funny," she said laughing. "We'll beat you all butts. The Wolfpack aren't in the same conversation with the Tar Heels. But I'll let you dream little boy."

We both laughed as I pulled into the circular driveway. I jumped out of the car quickly so I could open up her car door. She smiled as she stepped out, flashing that beautiful smile. We walked to the door and I before she could say anything, I kissed her gently on her lips. She hugged me and kissed me back. For some reason, I wasn't surprised. It felt unreal because I'd fantasized about this happening. I was beyond happy.

"I had an awesome time this evening!" I said softly. "Stay sweet!"

"I did too. It was beyond awesome. Spectacular. Fantastic." She said smiling. "Call me to let me know you made it home safely."

"Of course I will," I said. "Good bye beautiful."

I ran back to the car and sped off like I were a NASCAR driver. But I pulled over shortly to vomit. I felt much better after it was over, but now feeling the effects of chemotherapy. I drove home tired but happy, wondering if kissing Ezra was just a fling or something permanent. I had no know idea, pretty much like cancer: I had idea what would happen.

End of Chapter

I texted Ezra as soon as I got home. I had never wanted to text someone so badly like I wanted to text Ezra. Over excited was an understatement.

Me: Hey beautiful. I'm home. Once again I enjoyed myself. You're definitely a joy to be around.

Ezra: "Thanks. Glad you made it home safely. I enjoyed myself too. It's one of the best times I've ever had in my life. Thank you again for showing me a great time. You're really a great guy".

I showed my confidence. I wanted her to see me as confident instead of someone with cancer.

Me: "Welcome! Ezra. This is just the beginning of great things to come. We'll definitely do this again or something better. Life is short. Must enjoy it while we can."

What was I thinking when I made that statement? I thought to myself. I mentioned death and I had cancer. I was delusional. That statement could make her sad. Boy was I dumb. I worried myself thinking she would get upset.

Ezra: "Absolutely. We must enjoy life while we can. But think positive always, no need to focus on the negative. Thinking negative will only drain you. Think positive and great things will happen."

Me: "You're right. You're absolutely right. Must think positive. Anyway, goodnight beautiful woman. Sweet dreams".

Ezra: Always think positive. And Goodnight Mr. Handsome."

I texted a smiling face emoji. She texted me a kissing emoji with a heart. That text alone almost killed me because I was convinced she liked me. I fell asleep with my cell phone on my chest. That was a happy moment I must say.

I woke up early the next morning excited, although I felt queasy. Knowing that Ezra liked me gave me confidence. It wasn't the confidence of having a girl like me, but of facing and dealing with cancer. Although my attitude was still negative, Ezra and Jericho made me feel special, made me feel like I could beat cancer. But I only felt like that around them, no one else, including Mom. And Mom was a God fearing woman. I received positive vibes from Mom, too, but it was different compared to Ezra and Jericho. I knew they were special. There was a reason I met them, too.

Since I was exempt from school, my days consisted of chemotherapy, volunteering at the Animal Shelter, going to support group and now I was volunteering at the UNC Hospital, where Jericho received his chemotherapy treatments. Today was the first day. I knew Jericho was expecting me, and I wasn't about to let my little buddy down. I took my meds and showered. And I texted Ezra, wishing her a good morning. I had to make sure I stayed out of the friend zone, although we had kissed. After I showered, I put on some black dress pants, a black leather shoes, a red, long sleeved dress shirt, and a white bow tie with a Wolfpack emblem. I was going to represent NC State Wolfpack, especially at UNC Hospital. Remember, UNC Tar Heels and NC State Wolfpack was big time rivals.

Mom cooked me some eggs and prepared me a big bowl of fruit, consisting of strawberries, blueberries, pineapples, and bananas. I ate all of the fruit and drank three glasses of orange juice. Then I had drunk three bottles of water. I had to drink plenty of water to stay hydrated. Chemo drained the body like the desert sun. I needed water like a fish.

I noticed Mom kept looking at me smiling. It was a sneaky grin. I knew what that meant. She wanted to talk and ask me a thousand questions about last night with Ezra. I was glad I had somewhere to go because Mom would talk me to death. So I looked at her and waited for a response.

"Well Paul, my handsome son, you look sharp today. If I didn't know any better, I'd say you were going to preach a sermon," she said grinning. "How did your date go last night with Ezra? I'm sure you have a lot to talk about it."

I grinned and shook my head like an innocent child. Actually, I blushed. "It was nice Mom, but I want to thank you for yacht ride at the lake. That was very special of you Mom," I said, giving her a big hug. "We had an awesome time Mom. She truly enjoyed herself. But Mom I have to go now. Remember, I'm volunteering at the UNC Children's Hospital today. I'm going to see Jericho."

"Oh that's right! I forgot," said Mom, who hardly ever forgets anything. "Paul that's very nice of you to devote your time and energy to a great cause. You'll be a blessing to someone. Believe that."

"Thanks Mom," I said and kissed her on the forehead.

"Make sure you eat something and drink plenty of water and juice," said Mom. "And how are you feeling because I can drive you if you want me to."

"I always drink plenty of water and I'm okay Mom," I said, feeling like she wanted to baby me.

"Okay. Drive safely," she said.

"I will Mom. Promise," I said.

My stomach was queasy but I wasn't about to tell Mom because she would want to drive me there and feed me like a baby and stuff. I understood Mom loved me and I appreciated her for loving me so much.

But wasn't the type that wanted to be cuddled and wrapped up like a blanket. I was 17 years old and living with cancer and felt bad, a funk I tried to shake every waking moment. Being pampered was an ugly reminder. But I was going to visit my little buddy Jericho. I was looking forward to that. For whatever reason, Jericho made me feel good.

I wanted to make a great impression on my first visit, so I wrote a script on what I should say and do. I rehearsed the script in my head as I drove the 30 minute trip to Chapel Hill. I planned to say, *Hello My name is Paul Christian and I'm here volunteering with the cancer patients today. I'm going to read to them and talk to them.* When I rehearsed it loudly, it sounded cheesy, like I was kissing up to someone. Anyway, my goal was to sound professional and educated. So I thought it sounded okay, although cheesy. The drive was boring and longer than I anticipated. But that changed when I received a call from Jericho. He wanted to know if I were still coming.

Jericho: "Hey man, how far are you? You know I've told the other kids about you and they're excited. So don't let us down." He started laughing, loudly.

Me: "Man I'm about 10 minutes away. Hold tight little buddy. I'll be right there. I'm a man of my word, remember. Plus, I owe you a butt whipping from the last time you beat me in **NBA 2k 16.** You're going down my brother." I laughed hard, knowing he'll kick my butt easily.

Jericho: "Keep dreaming Paul. There's nothing wrong with dreaming. We're all dreamers. Ha!Ha!" He was laughing historically.

I swear Jericho acted like a grown man, almost like a grandfather. Or he had the spirit of a grandparent. This kid was wise beyond his years, as if he came from another time. I was ready to see him, though. So I drove a faster, not to fast though. Mom would lose her mind if I received a speeding ticket. I got to UNC Children's hospital faster than I expected and found good parking. Basically, I found good parking because I had a special placard given to me by UNC Hospital as volunteer. UNC Hospital was huge, everything was in Carolina Blue, yuck I thought to myself. I took the elevator to the third floor and checked in with the reception. I explained who I was and she told me they were expecting me. She handed me sign a confidentiality form along with information about me. As I filled out the form, I couldn't help but look at all of the pictures of the young children who suffered from cancer. There were pictures of toddlers who had cancer. They were all smiling, with doctors and nurses surrounded by them. Some pictures were of the parents playing with their children. In all of the pictures, the children were happy. I wondered how could they smile when they were suffering. Well I was about to see it firsthand.

A few minutes later, someone tapped me on my shoulder. I turned around and I didn't see anyone. When I turned my head back around, Jericho jumped out of nowhere and said "Boo!" He scared me so bad I fell out of the chair. And Jericho laughed so hard he was crying, and so were the other kids. All I could do was shake my head and laugh with them.

"You got me real good Jericho!" I said laughing. "I see I have to be careful around you. Man you're something else."

"Of course, that's the only way to live. Scaring people to death, enjoying life," said Jericho. "Making people laugh helps them, makes them healthy. Laughter is good for the soul."

"So I guess you're a doctor now!" I said laughing.

"Yeah, I am. You can call me that," said Jericho laughing. "I wish you could've seen the expression on your face man. It was priceless. Wish I had recorded it. I would 've put that on YouTube."

"Yeah it was too funny. I'll get you back when you least expect it. Oh payback is terrible my brother," I said laughing loudly.

"Whatever Paul! You have to wake up early to catch me off guard," said Jericho. "I'll get you again before the days over."

"You probably will," I said shaking my head and smiling at the same time. Jericho was an awesome kid, loveable. By now, Ms. Ruth had showed up and gave me my volunteer badge. My name was printed in huge black letters with a Carolina Blue background. Ms. Ruth was very sweet.

"Glad you could make it Paul. We really appreciate it when people come and volunteer their time, especially teenagers," said Ms. Ruth. "They look forward to people spending time with them. Thank you Paul."

"You're very welcome Ms. Ruth. I really want to be here to support the children and the teenagers. They're dealing with a deadly disease.

They need all of the support they can get," I said with a serious tone. And I really felt that way. Although I wasn't the most positive thinking person with cancer, I knew these children needed support all types of support. And I was going to do my part.

Since I was friends with Jericho, Ms. Ruth asked if I'd like to work with his group. His group consisted of two girls and two other boys, making it a group of five. They were very frail but happy. They smiled all of the time. Their names were Queen, Warmeta, Bill, and Henry. They were younger than Jericho, ages 10 and 11. There were other volunteers there, too. But they were older than me, like in their late twenties or early thirties. We were going to visit a bird sanctuary, owned by some millionaire, who loved to help children with cancer. It was a short drive to the sanctuary from the hospital, according to Ms. Ruth. We hopped on the blue bus and I talked to Jericho and the rest of the gang. They asked me all types of questions, mainly about basketball. Of course, Jericho was the leader, so he leaned back in the seat and let the others take turns asking me questions. Jericho was one cool dude.

"So do you dunk the basketball all the time?" asked Queen, who was so adorable. "Whose your favorite basketball team? I bet you can't beat my Daddy in basketball."

"I dunk every time I can," I joked.

"How tall are you? And your feet are big. They look like little canoes!" said Warmeta, who laughed so hard she was crying. "I bet you can sail on water with those big feet."

"Your feet are big, but do you think you can show me how to play basketball?" asked Bill. "I bet if you show me how to play basketball, I'll be good like Carmelo Anthony. He's my favorite player. Do you think you can beat Carmelo Anthony?"

"I'd love to show you how to play basketball. I'm way better than Carmelo Anthony!" I said jokingly about Carmelo Anthony, who played for the New York Knicks and one of the best basketball players in the NBA. He was an NBA Superstar.

"You all know he can't beat no Carmelo Anthony in basketball!" said Henry, who pointed at me and started laughing. "He'll kill you and dunk all on you Paul. He'll dunk on you so hard; he'll knock the 'P' off of your name. And he'll cross you up and break your ankles."

I had to laugh at that comment. It was too funny. He was a little comedian. I loved the conversation, joking with them and everything. You would never believe they were suffering from cancer.

"I'll break Carmelo Anthony's ankles on the basketball court. I'll cross him up, spin around and dunk it. He'll know I'm the best!" I joked, waiting for them to gang up on me.

"You know you can't even dunk. You probably can't even touch the rim. All of that height and you can't do anything but lie to young kids!" joked Jericho, who had everyone laughing now, including Ms. Ruth and the bus driver. "How can anyone slam dunk with those big canoe feet? I'm afraid you might kick someone in the head and kill them! Paul you made the basketball team because the coach felt sorry for you."

I fell out laughing. Jericho was too funny. He knew how to captivate an audience and get their attention. Everyone looked at Jericho as if he was a stand-up comic. I enjoyed it joking with all of them. I made it a point to get Jericho excited.

"Jericho I could beat LeBron James in a game of one on one. He's no match for me and my big, canoe feet," I joked, which made everyone laugh, because everyone knew LeBron James was the best basketball player in the world, not just the NBA. "I'll dunk on LeBron so hard his hairline will move back." Everyone burst out laughing, especially Jericho, who laughed so hard he was slobbering from the mouth. "Yeah, that's what I'll do. I'm a bad man."

"That's a good one Paul! Well at least LeBron has a hairline. We don't. Well we used to have one before Mr. Cancer took away!" joked Paul, referring to being bald headed because of cancer. "It'll grow back or I'll just paint a hairline on my head."

Everyone cracked up laughing. It was too funny. All of his friends held their stomachs laughing, slapping their hands on the bus seats.I laughed so hard I thought I was going to piss on myself.

"Jericho you're a little comedian," I joked. "You can make the Devil laugh."

"The Devil isn'tno match for a boy like me!" joked Jericho. "I'll have the Devil wanting to get back into Heaven."

We all laughed again. He had the whole bus laughing at him. And all of his friends were hyping him up to keep joking. They were all happy, smiling like they were healthy children. I wondered how did they get that way. What was their secret? Heck, Jericho was so confident and positive you wondered if he really had cancer. Of course, he had cancer, but he paid cancer no attention. He acted like it wasn't there. He treated cancer like a side dish, a side dish he would throw away at a moment's notice. Jericho acted like cancer had him, not the other way around.

We pulled up to the bird sanctuary. It was located on an100 acre farm, which was written a blue and white sign. **Welcome to Smith Estates, home of the largest bird sanctuary in America**. A huge white mansion witha manicured yard sat at the front of the entrance. The farm was separated from the mansion, probably like a mile away. Before we could even get onto the property, the bus driver was met at the gate by a big, muscular security guard. The security guard came to the driver's window. The bus driver, who was an older gentleman, showed the security guard his badge and the gates opened.

The steel-ironed gates were about 12 feet high with sharp arrows at the top. Cameras sat on top of a several light poles. It seemed more like a high security prison than a residence with a bird sanctuary, despite the beautiful mansion and acres of farm land. The farm was beautiful, but I had never seen a farm with paved roads. I thought farms had dusty, dirty roads. Whoever owned this farm was beyond a millionaire. Maybe he was a billionaire because the farm looked more like a miniature city instead a farm. There were acres of rolling green grass that stretched as far as an ocean. Several miniature brick builds were on a steep hill. Horses,cows, goats, chickens, rabbits, and other animals I'd never seen before wereon the farm. Plenty of children played with the animals or interacted with them. There was an adult or two with them. I assumed they must have been volunteers like me.

Several miniature brick buildings were on a steep hill. I assumed that's where we were heading to. The bus drove up the steep, winding road towards the brick buildings. We finally made it to the bird sanctuary. It was located on another acre of land witha circular drive way and a statue of an eagle in the front. The sanctuary had the most beautiful view. You could see the entire mansion and farm, along with the beautiful forest and lake. It looked as if someone had painted nature and placed it there. You could see the birds flying high in the blue sky, hovering over the hills and forest. The birds flew in the sky as if they knew they were surrounded by wealth. Jericho was super excited.

"Alright, everyone! Let's go save our children. Let's remind them that all isn't lost. They will recover. There is hope," said Jericho, referring to the birds in the sanctuary.

And Jericho had all of his friends hyped, too. They followed him instead of Ms. Ruth, who was laughing with the rest of them. We entered the bird sanctuary and were greeted by the staff, who led us to a large auditorium full of different types of birds. Information about the bird was printed on a sign, like its origin, what part of the world it came from, the birds eating habits, its enemies and so much more. It reminded me of being in a museum, where the information about the dinosaur was written on a card.

Everyone was assigned a staff member. We were in group of threes, the staff member, Jericho and myself. Jericho knew the routine, wash your hand, put on gloves and wear a pair scrubs. It was the type of scrubs doctors wore.

"We're about to have some fun Paul!" said Jericho excitedly, scrubbing his hands as if he were about to perform an operation.

"Yeah he's a great-leader, very intelligent," said the staff member, an older gentleman by the name of Isaiah, who specialized in treating birds. Basically, the staff were trained Avian Veterinarian. Avian Veterinarians specialized in treating all types of birds, including exotic birds. Jericho's favorite bird was the sparrow. He loved sparrows. In fact, he and Ms. Ruth were working on a Sparrow at the Wildlife Rehabilitation Center.

"Hey there Ikey. My little Ikey!" said Jericho, referring to the sparrow and rubbing the feathers of Ikey. "He's getting better Mr. Isaiah. Looks like his wings are healing. And he's grown."

"Yes he has. Look at his feet," said Mr. Isaiah. "He's on the mend. But he's eating so much. We changed his diet and are expecting him to fully recover."

"I can see. So we can I wash him, clean him up and feed him?" asked Jericho.

"Sure!" said Mr. Isaiah.

"Let's go then! I'm ready!" said Jericho.

"Okay! Cool!" said Mr. Isaiah.

"I can help, too," I said joking.

"You're going to help me do everything!" said Jericho, laughing.

"Alright!"I said smiling. "Let's do it!" I was hyped, too. I had never done anything with a bird before.

We grabbed a grey tub and filled it up with an antibiotic, liquid soap. We put Ike in the soapy water and he relaxed. Jericho and I started scrubbing Ike softly. He chirped softly, making direct eye contact. I felt like a parent washing a baby.

"This is how you clean it Paul," explained Jericho, cleaning underneath the wing of the sparrow in a circular motion. "It makes him feel relaxed and comfortable. I believe it helps him heal better. The goal is to heal him so that he can fly again. When he flies again, he'll be free again."

"Absolutely!" I said, agreeing with Jericho.

"See, if this bird doesn't get fixed, he'll never fly again. And if can't fly, he can't feed himself. If he can't feed himself, then he can't survive. That means he'll die," explained Jericho, continuing to clean Ike, and express his logic.

"Makes a lot of sense," I said, still trying to figure out how a 13-year old could be so smart. "Jericho, can I ask you a question?"

"What caused you to love birds so much?" I asked.

"When I was about five or six years old, I found a bird in our back yard that was hurt and couldn't fly. I picked him up and showed him to Dad and Mom. I asked them could I keep him and take care of it. They were against it at first, but they let me keep it. Dad took it to a vet to make sure it received the proper care. The vet fixed him and told us what we needed to do to keep him. But since it was a regular bird, the vet said we should let it go once it was healed. So every day I washed him, fed and talked to him. I gave him the proper food and everything. Of course, Dad was right there to help me. After a few weeks, he was healed. I knew we had to let him go. We had to let him go, release him back into the wild. On the final day of keeping him, I bathed him and kissed him. Dad and I took him to the mountains and released him on one of the highest peaks. It was an amazing sight to see him fly away, wings flapping. I cried all the way home. Dad explained to me that when someone is healed, be a bird or a person, you are supposed to set it free.

Setting it free it allows it to live again. I'll never forget what Dad told me. He said when you truly love someone; you always set it free when the opportunity presents itself. I'll always remember that." And that's why I love birds."

I nodded my head and stood in silence for a few minutes before saying anything. Jericho was very intelligent, and I never wanted to sound stupid talking to him. Never.

"That is an interesting way to fall in love with a bird. What an amazing story. It doesn't get any better than that. I love how your parents let you keep the bird and ~~they~~ your dad helped you take care of it," I said, still in amazement at his story. "I love that saying about whenever you love someone or something, you set it free."

"Yep!" said Jericho. "I'm going to be an Avian Veterinarian one day. I'm going to go to North Carolina State University to become a veterinarian. I just love birds, all types of birds. Eagles, parrots, robins, cardinals, ravens, even like buzzards. It's amazing how God created a species that can fly, soar as high as an airplane and then come back down to earth. That is amazing. So I'm learning all I can about birds now. Because, I want to save all of the birds in the world."

"I believe you'll do it little buddy!" I said excitedly.

"Absolutely!" he said back smiling, as he poured more antibacterial soap on the bird. "It's my mission to become one, to rescue birds, heal birds and to give them a better way of life."

I didn't know if I were talking to a 13 year old or an old man with career goals. Jericho impressed me each and every time. The more time I spent with him, the more I realized he was very intelligent and positive minded. He was beyond his years. I knew teenagers who didn't speak or talk as intelligent as Jericho. Heck, I wasn't as smart as this young teenager.

"Well what about your cancer? Are you worried about it stopping you from going to college and becoming an Avian Veterinarian?" I asked, and regretting as soon as I said it. Man was I dumb for asking that stupid question. I knew I had cancer because I had said the stupidest thing ever. "I'm sorry Jericho; I didn't mean to say that! Say it like that! Stupid of me!"

"It's okay Paul! You didn't mean any harm," said Jericho, assuring me that I wasn't the fool I thought I was. "I understand exactly what you meant, but actually, that's a great question to ask someone. Like I said before, cancer is the boogeyman, but I'm the superhero. I refuse to give cancer the strength to kill me or defeat me. I won't allow it to. It's a side dish, a side item, something I don't need or should have. Cancer can only motivate me. Not hinder me. I will never give cancer the power over me. If I give it the power over me, then will kill me. It will kill my spirit. But as long as I have the power over cancer, I'll defeat it. Never give in to cancer. Giving in to cancer is losing. I cannot and will not let cancer take away my dreams. Cancer is an obstacle. A hurdle. A bump in the road. It's an ugly disease that will slow you down. But you can't let it slow you down and stop you from dreaming. Always remember that. The power over cancer is our battle cry."

I was speechless. It felt like I had heard a motivational speaker. I was hyped to say the least. I was motivated, too. I wanted to feel what Jericho was feeling. He treated cancer like it was irrelevant, as if it was a worrisome knot. I stood in admiration of this young kid, who had the confidence and determination that I lacked. I fronted about having cancer, but in reality, I was scared as hell, scared of dying. But I wanted to get to the place of Jericho, where cancer was irrelevant, where it was nonexistent, and a side dish.

"I'm going to keep that in mind Jericho. That is the best way to be," I said, still in awe of Jericho's confidence. "I just don't understand how you operate the way you do. Wish I could do that."

Jericho continued to wash the bird and looked up at me and smiled.

"It's in you to do it. It's in you to conquer cancer. It's in there Paul!" said Jericho, pointing at his heart. "You have to believe in yourself to find it, to believe you can do it. I found it because I saw my father fight it. He kept going, kept working, never allowing it to defeat him. The dream must be bigger than letting cancer kill you."

"I respect what you're saying. I just don't know if I can find it," I said, still trying to wrap my head around this subject. "I have no idea how to find it, how to have a positive attitude while having cancer. I will say that I'm interested in finding it. I need to find it."

"You will find it Paul! You'll find it when you least it expect it!" said Jericho, who was smiling from ear to ear. "Everything happens for a reason Paul. You having cancer happened for a reason. The same with me, too. But what is the reason? Who knows what the reason is. But I've found peace and happiness in healing birds and taking care of them. And I'm always happy. Everyone's situation is different, but I'm only speaking about my experience. I happen to love my experience because I know my purpose."

"That's what I mean. It's so complicated. I will never understand how someone can be so happy and content living with cancer," I said, as I helped Jericho wash Ikey. "But I believe it to be a wonderful thing. I really do. It's something I'm going to strive for. I really am."

"I want to see you strive for it, just like you do in basketball. You had to strive to be good a great basketball player. You have to work on dunking a ball," explained Jericho. "You did all of that without cancer. You became a great basketball player without ever thinking you would have cancer. So why would you stop achieving your goals now that you have cancer? Keep asking yourself that question and you'll find your answer."

I felt like a student listening to the teacher. A 13 year old was encouraging me how to deal with cancer instead of the other way around.

"I'll do exactly that!" I said, shaking my head. "I've never looked at it that way. It's a different way to look at having cancer. It's an approach I have to use."

By now, everyone was listening to our conversation, including Mr. Isaiah. Actually, it was more like Jericho was giving a speech about how to beat cancer. Queen, Warmeta, Bill, and James raised their hands as if they were in class. And Jericho pointed to Queen.

"I just want to say that was the first thing I saw in you was your positive attitude. You always did what you wanted to do and paid the cancer no mind," recalled Queen. "Then you took the time to be my friend when I didn't have any friends. You're positive attitude is why I've been able to deal with cancer."

"Thank you Queen!" said Jericho. "You're a great person Queen."

"Yep! That's why I liked coming to the hospital because I knew Jericho would make me feel better!" said Warmeta, who gave Jericho a hug. "You're the best Jericho. You always brought me something to drink after my chemotherapy and a video game to play. I will always remember that."

"You introduced me to these birds and told me to concentrate on that," said Bill, who was scrubbing the feathers of his bird. "You said a positive attitude was the best medicine."

"Yeah he told me the same thing about having a positive attitude," said James, agreeing with Bill. "That meant a lot to me, especially after I had surgery and didn't think I would ever have any friends. And you became my friend Jericho."

I thought I was witnessing an episode of the "Oprah Winfrey" show. Everyone loved Oprah because her shows were awesome and legendary, always talking about a great topic. Topics that made you cry a real tear jerker. The only person missing from this conversation was Oprah Winfrey herself. And Mr. Isaiah eyes watered. It was obvious the topic was getting to him. Jericho had single handedly inspired a group of children with cancer.

"Thanks to all of you. Thank you so much!" said Jericho, who gathered all of them and hugged them. "You all are my friends and I love you dearly. Cancer brought us together but surviving and beating cancer is the bond that will allow us to love each other forever."

"That's right Jericho!" they all yelled at the same time, hugging each other in a circle.

"My buddy Jericho!" said James.

"We love you man!" said Bill.

"You're right about that!" said Queen.

"Glad we're all friends!" said Warmeta.

"This is absolutely wonderful! What a display of friendship," said Mr. Isaiah, who was dapping his eyes with Kleenex. "I've never seen a friendship like the one you all share."

Of course, I was the one lost for words. I was surprised at the level of positivity and friendship. They acted with a level of maturity you see in adults. I was supposed to act in this manner, not think negative. My behavior and mindset about cancer was childish, at best. And my mind wondered what to say. I couldn't be the only one silent.

"What a special group of kids! The positivity you all have is awesome. I hope to be like y'all one day and not think about having cancer," I said, trying not to sound cheesy, but wanting to have something valuable to say. However, I enjoyed the experience and felt special. "This is something I didn't expect but I'm happy to witness it."

"We're happy to have you here Paul! And you'll get the positive attitude!" said Jericho.

"I'll do my best!" I said. "I have too."

"You will!" said Jericho.

Man I hope so, I thought to myself.

After we had our emotional chat, Mr. Isaiah reminded everyone how he appreciated working with them and that they all were brave and strong. He thanked me for volunteering, too, wishing me well with my fight with cancer. He made sure that I understood that my volunteering really helped the group today. He said he'd never seen a group of children have a deep and positive conversation about cancer. We all thanked him, each one of us giving him a high five.I personally told him how I enjoyed the experience.

By now, we had washed up Ikey and the rest of the birds. Ikey was so clean he resembled a new born sparrow. He was jet black and beautiful. Jericho finished brushing down his feathers and kissed him. We sat Ikey back in his cage and washed our hands thoroughly. Ikey looked so sad, though. He chirped loudly as we all left the building.

"I'll be back buddy. I love you!" said Jericho. Ikey chirped louder and louder, as if he knew what Jericho was talking about. "He's a good bird. Man I already misses him."

"You'll see him tomorrow at the Wildlife Rehabilitation Center," said Mr. Isaiah.

"Yes you certainly will!" said Ms. Ruth, who had rejoined our group, giving everyone a gift basket full of fruit.

"Yeah I know!" said Jericho.

"We'll see him tomorrow buddy," I said.

"We sure will," said Jericho.

When everyone turned their back, I looked up and pointed my finger towards the sky, and said, "Dad, can I really beat cancer? Can I defeat it?" Then I walked slowly back to the bus.

When I got home, I noticed I had several missed text messages from Ezra. I had so much fun at the sanctuary I had forgotten to text her back. And I really liked Ezra. But I was tired and nauseated. But I was so happy to see that she texted me. It had been over two hours. What was I thinking? I texted her back immediately.

Ezra: "Hey Paul. I hope you're having a great da. I'm know Jericho is enjoying himself."

Me: "Hello beautiful. I'm sorry for the late response…got wrapped up with Jericho and the kids. Yes I had a great day. Yes, he had a great time. We all had a great time. How was your day?"

Ezra: "Hey there! It's okay, no need to apologize for enjoying yourself. I thought Jericho had kidnapped you! LOL! You know he loves sparrows. I'm surprised he didn't talk you to death."

Me: "I enjoy hanging out with Jericho. He's such a positive young boy. And he's so funny. What more can you ask for. I love spending time with Jericho. He's my buddy. I'm learning so much from him."

Ezra: "That's great Paul! Me and Mom really appreciate you being his friend. That means the world to us. All he does is talk about you and how you and hanging out with you. I want you to know that he really likes you. He looks up to you Paul! We thank you so much for the time you spend with Jericho!"

Me: "Well you are certainly welcome! You and the whole family! He's just special. That's the best way I can put it and I enjoy every opportunity with him. I learn something new every time we're together."

Ezra: "Well thank you again Paul. We really appreciate it. It warms my heart to know how much my little brother likes you. He's special, but so are you Paul. I don't think you realize it. And I don't think you understand the impact you have on Jericho."

Me: "You're very welcome. It's a pleasure."

Ezra: "You're such a sweetie! A genuine sweetheart!"

Me: "You're the sweetheart!"

Ezra: "Here is a kiss for you!"

Actually, Ezra texted me an emoji with kisses. That blew me away. I was beyond happy. I texted her same type of emoji, except mine had hearts and kisses.

Me: "Thanks for the emoji. I like that!"

Ezra: "You're welcome. You deserve it."

Me: "I enjoyed talking to you. I'm about to go to bed. I will hit you tomorrow baby girl. Enjoy your night."

Ezra: "Goodnight handsome! I enjoyed you!"

And Ezra texted me an emoji with a heart.I smiled that night. I smiled for different reasons, though. Mentally, I was in a good place, and I made up my mind to think positive, very positive about having cancer. I thought long and hard about what Jericho had said. His message was positive. I wanted to be positive. Dad was positive. I was going to be positive, no matter how hard the fight. And I was going to beat it. That was a promise!

I slept like a baby that night. But I had a weird dream. It was an eerie dream, surreal to be honest. I was playing a basketball game for the NC State Wolfpack, and we were playing against a team dressed in black, even the socks were black. I couldn't see the name of team. But they wore the poison symbol across their jersey. They had no faces, just a huge circle with dark eyes that constantly moved. What amazed me was that they had so many players on the court at the same time. How in the world could I play against so many players, I thought to myself. There had to be at least a hundred of them! They were scary looking because they all joined together like a chain linked fence and grew. It seemed like a big glob or a thousand bees! And I had the ball dribbling up the court. It was just me, no teammates or anything, not even a coach. I was all by my lonesome. However, there were thousands of fans cheering me on, clapping loudly. But they were off in a long distance. But the funny part was that I could see all of my family and friends, just cheering, jumping up and down. They were screaming loudly, but I could hear the chant, "you can beat them! Beat them! Beat them! You can do it!" Then I heard a familiar voice, a loud booming voice. I looked around and it was Dad, cheering me on. "You can do it! Don't give up! Don't ever give up!" Suddenly, I heard another familiar voice. I looked around and saw Jericho, sitting beside Dad, yelling and clapping. "Come on Paul! You can do this! You got it my man!" With all of the cheering going on, my confidence grew like a flower. Six seconds was left on the shot clock. And I was at the half court. So I dribbled the ball, faked out a few players, kept dribbling the ball and shot the ball…that's all I remembered about the dream. I never understood the meaning of the dream, not yet anyway. But the dream was a sign of things to come. Honestly, it was a premonition, something I never understood. In due time, I understood the meaning.

The next morning, I had my regular scheduled chemo appointment along with a visit at the Wildlife Rehabilitation Center. But I had a severe headache and was very nauseated. I rushed to the bathroom and vomited, but I vomited blood. I knew something was wrong, very wrong. I tried to stand up but fell back down hard on the floor, reaching for the toilet as leverage to pull myself back up. I got back up and vomited some more, still heaving blood and other junk. I wanted to scream for Mom, but my voice wouldn't allow it. It was hollow. Then again, I remembered how I didn't want Mom to worry. So I remained calm, thinking the vomiting would go away. But it wasn't going to go away. I was in too much pain. Blood was everywhere and I was becoming weak by the minute. My stomach started rumbling like a volcano. I felt like someone dropped a 100 pound block on my stomach and chest. My vision blurred, air escaped my lungs and blood gushed out my mouth. Then the lights faded. It was darkness. I passed out.

I heard familiar voices, but I still saw darkness. It felt like I was dreaming because remained closed and I was lying down. I tried hard to open my eyes but nothing happened. I tried to move my legs and arms, nothing happened. I turned my head; it wouldn't move. I was confused. My body felt paralyzed. I panicked. I screamed. But nothing came out. And the people with the familiar voices continued to talk. *Was I dead? Was I dying I thought.* Slowly and slowly, I started putting the voices with the faces. I heard Mom's voice but couldn't actually make out what she was saying. Her words were muffled, as if she were crying. I realized she was talking to Dr. John, my doctor who oversees my chemotherapy. I strained my ears to hear but it stayed the same. Then I heard nothing but silence. I fell back to sleep because I dreamt I was playing basketball and I heard no voices. I wasn't sure if I was sleep or not. I remembered zoning in and out. One minute I heard voices, the next minute I was counting lizards, not sheep. Or I could feel myself sweating and someone gently wiping the sweat off of my forehead. It was back and forth like a yo-yo. I wasn't able to open my eyes but I stayed nauseated, on the verge of throwing up. It was like my body had mind of its own. Maybe I was dying and didn't know it. Then the familiar voices returned. But this time around, I heard them more clearly.

"His blood pressure is rising, pulse is getting better. His temperature is better, too. I'm going to make sure he has enough oxygen," said a woman with a soft voice, a familiar voice. I strained my ears to hear more of the conversation and to put a face with the voice.

"It looks like the antibiotics are working," said a man with a booming voice. He sounded like Dr. John, but I wasn't sure. And I still couldn't open my eyes or mouth, nor could I feel my body.

"Make sure you add the IV salt solution. This will continue to improve his blood pressure," said the man I believed to be Dr. John.

"It's already in there," said the woman with the soft voice.

"Great! I'm waiting for the results of his blood culture. That way we'll know the specific identity of the bacteria," said the man I believed to be Dr. John.

"He's doing so much better than when he arrived," said the woman with the soft voice.

"That's a good thing!" said the man I believed to be Dr. John. "Just waiting for him to regain conscience."

I was beyond shock. What had happened to me? How was I able to hear them but couldn't wake up or move my body? This was crazy. This confused me to the point that I could feel my heartbeat thump through my chest. I wanted to cry, but nothing happened. What kind of physical state was I in? I felt like a kid in a haunted house all by himself. It was a matter of time before the monster jumped out of the closet and killed me. And what happened next was like a death blow. I wasn't prepared for it.

"He's in a comatose like state right now. We believe he'll come through because his blood pressure is getting better and his vital signs are getting better. From my experience, patients have a good chance of coming out of the comatose like state," said the doctor.

"Thank you so much! That's the best news I've heard Dr. John!" said a woman who sounded just like my mom. I replayed her voice in my head. That was my Mom! I'm sure that was Mom. And that was Dr. John. I became excited.

"You're very welcome Mrs. Christian!" said Dr. John. "Any questions, feel free to ask. That's what I'm here for."

"I really appreciate that!" I heard Mom say.

And I was right! Mom was there! She was there.

I was in a comatose state, I thought to myself! What was happening? How was I in a comatose state but could still hear people talk? And why wasn't there any feeling in my legs, arms or anything? Why couldn't I open up my eyes? These were the questions running through my mind. Maybe I was dreaming, after all. But was it possible to hear people while in a comatose state? After that, I remembered nothing. I heard no voices or anything. I guess you can say I was in a deep sleep. I was just there. That had to be the case because all I did was sleep.

But one day, I regained the feeling in my body. I no longer felt numb. I felt the blood rushing in my legs, arms, stomach, my head, ears, feet, fingers, and just all over my body. Suddenly, I felt someone's hand on my shoulder. They squeezed it softly and whispered in my ear, "hey man, how are you? You're a tough Wolfpacker! Stop playing and wake up? We all know you're faking, not wanting to go to school!" he joked. I knew the voice, but I couldn't put a face with it because I was in too much pain and groggy. I tried hard to open my eyes but nothing happened. But he whispered in my ear again.

"Look, here big feet! Get your butt up! We're sitting around waiting for you to wake up and you're playing games! Don't you understand we've been here forever waiting on you to wake up!" he continued to joke. "And I'm hungry, heck we're all hungry. We understand you might not be hungry, but we're all tired of this hospital food. So wake up with your big, canoe feet!"

I recognized his voice immediately. It was Jericho, my buddy. I was shocked and surprised to know he was there. I was beyond happy! All of sudden I grinned and then I laughed. My eyes were still closed, but I must have laughed loudly because I heard other people say "he's laughing! He's laughing! It's a miracle! He's laughing! He's awake!"

I was awake, but I couldn't open my eyes yet. I opened up my mouth, but the words wouldn't come out. Then Mom said, "his mouth is opening up! He's trying to talk! Oh my God!"

I heard an Army of footsteps run towards my bed! They ran so fast that my bed shook. Everyone tried to talk at one time. It sounded like a football stadium full of screaming fans. I heard so many voices I thought everyone in the state of North Carolina was in my room! But I kept trying to open my eyes and mouth. As I tried to do both, I felt the sharp pain throughout my body. I thought I had been electrocuted by lighting. The pain was unbearable, especially when I tried to talk or move my body. I realized I was fully conscious because Dr. John said, "he feels the pain because he's feeling the pain. We'll put more pain medication in his IV!"

"That's awesome!" said Mom! "I've been up forever it seems like praying for him to regain consciousness. This is the best news ever! This cancer is awful! I thought Paul was going to die. I thought we lost him for good. That would've killed me, losing my husband and Paul… would've been too much to bear!"

"Well, I'm very happy he's alive! He's a fighter!" said Dr. John. "He fought through it."

There were others talking, but I wasn't concerned with them or what they were saying. I was in too much pain to think about Mom's comments, too! I focused on opening up my eyes. My eyelids felt paralyzed, like they were nailed down. I kept trying, while tuning out all of the chatter in the room! However, that didn't last long because Jericho made his presence known. He demanded my attention.

"Hey man! I know the pain you're feeling, I've been there, and you're a fighter," said Jericho, whispering in my ear softly. "But if you open up your eyes, maybe you, me, and Ezra and go see the Wolfpack play the Tar Heels. But if you stay sleep, then you can't come! I guess I'll take Scooter your dog to the game. Ha! Ha!"

I laughed loudly and thought about Ezra and the basketball game. I really liked her and saw Jericho as the little brother I never had. I took a deep breath and decided to go for it, opening my eyes. At that time, I strained really hard to open my eyes. Suddenly, they opened little by little like someone peeling back an orange. The bright lights blinded me as I raised up my hand to block it. My eyes were hurting because of the brightness. The lights appeared to be directly in my face. When my eyes were fully opened, everyone and everything looked blurry. I noticed a circle of people surrounded my bed, but making out their faces gave me a headache. Everyone was talking and clapping. They all tried talking to me at the same time, and they talked loudly. The louder they talked, the more my head hurt. I wanted to tell them all to be quiet, but I was in too much pain to do it. I tried to turn my head in the direction of the person speaking to me.

"Hey there Paul! My buddy!" said someone whose voice I didn't recognize.

"Paul, this is Mommy baby!" she said, gently rubbing my forehead. "I love you baby! I'm so blessed to see you up! Oh my God I love you! God is so good!"

I tried to speak, but nothing came out. All I could do was shake my head up and down. This was awful and then my body went limped. I felt paralyzed all over again, or at least it felt that way. Since my body was motionless and I couldn't feel anything, I felt the emotional pain driving through my body like a pitchfork. The pain was worse than actual tears. I wanted out. I wanted to die right then, take me out of my misery. The fear was real. I finally succumbed to the fact that I couldn't beat cancer. The fear was real because I could feel the tears stroll down my face. I closed my eyes and said a small prayer. I prayed so hard I caught a stomach cramp. But at that moment, a vision came upon me, a vision of my deceased Dad. Dad's face appeared out of nowhere. My goodness, there was Dad. Dad was there, just staring at me. What in the world was happening? I heard no other voices, only the image of my Dad, staring at me. It was as if my life had paused for a few minutes. Although I could no longer hear other people talking, I heard what my Dad said next. And it scared me.

"Paul, this is Dad. I know you're scared son, scared of dying, but now isn't the time to be scared. You have to be strong and fight it. Because, you can fight it. The fight is within you, but you have to find the fight. You cannot give up and lose the fight to cancer. I want you win this battle son. You can do it. You're a fighter! I've seen you fight all of your life. You did it as a premature baby! You beat it. You overcame being the shortest boy in class to being the tallest. You battled dyslexia and beat it because you were determined to read. You wanted to become a great basketball player, so you shot 1,000 jumpers a day until your arms hurt. You're a fighter Paul! You can beat cancer because fighting is in your blood! God didn't bring you this far to see you die! You're a

fighter and remember the Great Jim Valvano, never give up! Never give up son! Love you!"

Wow! That was amazing! I was in disbelief, totally shocked. Was I dreaming? Was Dad a ghost? Was I drugged up? I had just seen a vision of my Dad! My deceased father appeared in when I closed my eyes! I was happy and sad at the same time. There was happiness because I had just seen my Dad, but there was sadness because he was no longer here with me and Mom. My Dad was still dead. But would anyone ever believe me? Maybe I was hallucinating, after all; I'm sure the nurses doped me up with pain killers. I was really confused now because I was afraid to say anything to anyone. However, that pep talk gave me life, hope, and the will to live and beat cancer, once and for all. I'd forgotten about the struggles I had in my early childhood, and I had beaten all of them. Actually, I stored them away and never thought about them until I had a vision of Dad. My eyes remained closed, but the tears poured down my face like waterfalls. I took a deep breath and thought long and hard about what Dad said. Of course, I thought about the positive attitude of Jericho, and how he didn't let cancer defeat him. It wasn't going to defeat me either. I had too much to live for: my own life, Mom, Scooter, my affection for Ezra, and my new friend Jericho.

I gritted my teeth, bit down hard on my lip and used every strength in my body to move. It hurt like hell but I kept repeating in my head, "Never give up! Never give up! Never give up!" With every muscle fiber in my body, I moved my legs and arms and let out a loud gasp of air. My eyes were fully open and I saw everyone's facial expression! Everyone started clapping again. Mom kissed me and gave me the biggest hug. I could hardly breathe.

"Paul baby! I love you so much!" said Mom, kissing me all over my face.

"Hey man! Paul my buddy! So glad you made it through!" said Jericho, giving me a fist bump. "I miss you buddy! I prayed as hard as possible for you to make it through. My prayers were answered."

Then he leaned down in my ear and whispered and said softy, "Now that you're awake and feeling better, I'm going to kick your butt in NBA 2016 K! Ha-Ha!" I laughed so hard I felt no pain.

"We'll see! Just wait, I have magical powers now! You see I made it through his!" I joked.

"You're just delusional as always!" said Jericho, shaking my hand and patting me on my shoulder. "You're very famous, too, just look."

We both laughed and decided to play soon. By now, there was a crowd room of people waiting to say hello. There were people I hadn't seen in a long time, class mates, teammates, teachers, neighbors, church members, and the pastor of my church, cousins, and people from the Wildlife Rehabilitation Center. It amazed me so many people were there to see me. It seemed like I was a rock star, but only because I was sick. The conversations varied from silly and childish to real and caring.

"Paul we miss you dunking that basketball man and cracking jokes on everyone, especially about Bucktooth Billy! You know he still like fat girls!" said my teammate Joel. "Glad you're feeling better; we could certainly use you this season!"

"Yeah, thanks man!" I said, still shocked at what he said.

"It's so good to see you Paul, to see you pull through this situation. You're so strong. God gave you the strength to make it through. He has a purpose for you in life! You have a purpose Paul," explained Pastor Davis. "You're a living testimony of inspiration and fighting. You never gave up! God is good. We at the church are very proud of your other accomplishments, too!"

"Thanks Pastor Davis," I said shaking his large hand.

"Hey Paul! Glad you're doing okay!" said Mrs. Mary, an older lady and one of the church's senior deaconesses and one of my mother's friends. "We all prayed nonstop for you to make a full recovery."

"Thank You so much for your prayers and concerns," I said, extending my hand and kissing her on the cheek.

"My man Paul! Glad to see you buddy," said Coach Gomes, who gently shook my hand. "The whole team made a collage of you playing basketball and shooting game winning shots! We included pictures of you and all of your teammates! These are all happy moments we want you to remember. We all wrote you a warm, heartfelt letter, something special and meaningful from our hearts. We all want you to know how you have touched our hearts. You mean the world to us, especially to me. Love you Paul! Praying that you continue to finish the fight."

"Thank you so much Coach!" I said slowly and painfully, as the pain got worse.

"You're very welcome Paul!" said Coach Gomes. "Take care! See you soon!"

"Alright coach!" I felt like a rock star as the well-wishers continued to say nice things and give me high- fives. Although I was tired and in pain, the fact I had been comatose scared the living hell out of me and made me very appreciative of everyone. It was a teaching moment because I was learning the value of life, even though there were knuckle heads in the room, too.

"Man I thought you were going to die!" said Peter, a classmate of mine, who had no more sense than a squirrel. "Glad you made it through! Be glad when we can play basketball together for someone on!"

"Peter you're still crazy and stupid!" I mumbled under my breath and shook my head.

"My Mom and I left you a fruit basket over on the table! I left you some condoms too!" Peter joked. I wanted to punch him in the face for making me laugh. It hurt whenever I laughed.

"Thanks my man! Appreciate you coming by!" I said, waiting for everyone to leave so I could go back to sleep. On the other hand, I was enjoying them because I thought I was going to die. It was bittersweet because I had cancer, but I was living.

Then out of nowhere, all of my teammates circled around me and dapped me up, hugging me and giving me high fives. They surprised me big time. I was close to all of them, especially my main man Luke. Luke and I had played basketball together since we were five years old. I remembered how he used to destroy me on the basketball court, making me a better player. I wanted to cry but I held back the tears because I remembered the days of him pushing me to be a better basketball player. I could hear his voice now, "you better than me! Come on man, you can do it!"

"Paul my buddy! I've been praying for you! Praying hard for you! Thank God you came through! Love you!" said Luke, shaking my hand and hugging my neck at the same time. "You're tough man! I knew you would make it."

"Glad you came by my homeboy from back in the day!" I said, still holding his hand tightly.

"Yeah, I'm glad you think I'm tough because this cancer is kicking my ass man! It's no joke." "It may not be no joke, but I know you're a fighter! I know nothing stops Paul Christian! There is nothing you can't beat! I remember how hard you practiced until you could beat me and then you just destroyed me in basketball! Not only that, but you out grew me! I'm 6'1 and you're like 6'7! A giant!" said Luke, laughing.

"Yeah I remember those days very well!" I said softly, still fighting the pain and holding back the tears. I recognized cancer made me humble, very humble. I wanted to jump up and hug Luke and everyone in the room because I realized they loved me. They loved a teenage boy who could die of cancer. I prayed I wouldn't break down and cry.

"I'm going to go and let you get some rest," said Luke. "Take care man". I'll check on you later."

"Okayman!Take care my brother, thanks for coming to see me!" I said, giving him a fist bump.

Since there was a long line of well-wishers, everyone shook my hand and wished me well, except for a few people, like my teammates, who tried to cheer me up with laughter.

"I bet you have all the girls lining up to see you! Get sick and there they come running," joked my teammate Mark.

"Yeah Paul, all of the girls are talking about how good looking you are!" joked Amos, another teammate. "You're already the star basketball player in the state, and now you have every girl in Wake County after you."

"Whatever dude! I guess I had to get sick to really get their attention," I joked.

"Oh you definitely have all the women talking about you at school Paul! All of the pretty girls have been to the hospital to see you! That's a fact!" said Hosea, another teammate who was laughing historically.

"I cannot believe you guys." I said, "why do you all keep me laughing, making my ribs hurt. What do you guys want from me, all of this mess about the girls liking me?"

"It's true dude! The whole school is going nuts, especially the girls!" said King, another of my teammates. "You're the man!"

"Thanks but you guys are full of it!" I said, trying not to laugh.

In the moment, I thought about Ezra, wondering if she had abandoned me. I wasn't concerned about any other girls at school, glad they were concerned about my well- being. Other than that, I wanted to see Ezra.

"Well you may think I'm full of it, but that white bag over there is full of letters from all the pretty girls from school!" said King, who was laughing really hard. "I'll show you the letters. Watch this—"

"No, No!" I said, waving my hand to stop him, "I'll read it another time. I believe you. You guys being here is enough comfort for me! That's what matters the most, especially all of the jokes."

I wanted to get them out without being rude because I felt myself about to cry. I wasn't being ungrateful by any stretch. My thoughts pulled me in so many different directions and the pain was becoming unbearable. Mom sensed I wasn't feeling well because she summoned the nurse to give me some pain medication. That was a small sign and polite way to get people to leave. Then again, Mom wasn't afraid to ask people if need be. I knew Mom, could tell from her facial expressions she wanted me to get some rest.

"Paul, I'm going to put more pain medication in your IV. I see you grunting and what not," said the nurse. "This will make you feel better."

"Thank you!" I said.

"It will definitely make you sleeping, so everyone needs to finish up what they want to say because you'll be sleeping like a baby!" the nurse joked and referring to people in the room. "I'll make sure I give you enough to last several hours."

"That's awesome because I'm in so much pain! I can barely take it anymore," I said through grit teeth. "But I really wanted to see everyone." "No worries, do you want me tell everyone you need your rest?" the nurse asked.

"No that's okay. I'm going to enjoy them. I'll enjoy each and every one of them until the last one leaves," I whispered, not wanting anyone to hear me.

"Alright then, let me know if you change your mind," said the nurse softly.

"Thank you," I said.

"Welcome!" said the nurse.

By now, Mom came over and wanted to make sure I was okay. She was overly concerned, to be expected.

"Are you okay baby?" Mom asked. "I know you're tired and in pain. I can ask everyone to leave, just like the nurse said."

"It's okay Mom," I said. "I know how protective you can be, but I'm good. I'm happy, just thrilled to see all of my friends. They've uplifted my spirits so much."

"That's awesome Paul! Awesome!" said Mom excitedly, kissing me on my forehead. "I'll be right here baby."

"Cool," I said.

After talking to the nurse and Mom, I noticed Jericho talking to everyone, holding court like a judge. Everyone laughed loudly, as Jericho talked. He was very animated, waving his hands back and forth and exaggerating his movements, walking like Frankenstein. I had no idea what he was saying, but I knew it was about me because everyone kept looking in my direction, smiling. I found out soon enough.

"He could walk on water like Jesus with those big feet," said Jericho. "Be honest, his feet look like miniature canoes, sailing across Kerr Lake. He could loan his feet to an African safari and make money because they could use his feet as a canoe to kill alligators."All I heard was laughter. Non-stop laughter. I was fine with it because I even laughed, even though it made my chest hurt. Jericho was a funny dude. He knew how to take an awful situation and turn it into a fun one. He was one special dude, absolutely amazing. He was the brother I never had. I had to admit I was very close to him. He made me laugh, smile, and he gave me hope, hope to live. Jericho illustrated positivity. That's was my goal. He proved more than that at the hospital.

"You know what, he's very tired right now, though," Jericho said to the group of people. "He's being nice because he really enjoys all of us being here, but he's so tired. He's going to be dozing off soon. So let all of us say our good-byes and let Big Foot get some rest."

I laughed so hard I choked on the ice chips in my mouth, but it proved how much he cared about me. How in the world he knew I was tired was beyond me. I appreciated what he had done because I didn't want to seem ungrateful. Jericho was a life saver.

"Okay we'll definitely let him get some rest," said a female, who I didn't even know.

"Alright, we'll go say good-bye to him now," said Titus, one of my teammates. "Hey brother, praying for you. Hope you get better. And we'll win the championship for you! Go Eagles!"

"Thank you Titus, my brother. Appreciate you coming to check on me," I said. We dapped each other up with high-fives and promised to see each other when I was released. Everyone tried to say good-bye to me, however, the nurse told everyone to step out because they needed to examine me. That was good timing because I needed the rest. But I found out it was something different.

"Nothing is wrong Paul," said the nurse, smiling, "your friend Jericho wanted me to say that so that everyone could leave the room. That way you'll get your well- deserved rest."

"Really?" I said smiling and shaking my head at what Jericho had done. "He's one funny dude and I appreciate him doing that."

"Well he's definitely a good friend," said the nurse.

"Yes, he is," said Mom, who was standing beside the nurse. "He's a really nice kid. I like him."

"Where is he?" I asked. "I want to thank him, talk to him."

"He left already, but he left you a letter, though!" said Mom, smiling. "Go ahead and read it."

"That's okay Mom. I'll read it later because I'm so sleepy," I said.

"Okay sugar plumbs," said Mom, kissing my forehead. "I'm going to get a snack from the cafeteria, but I'll be right back."

"Alright Mom," I said, drifting off to sleep. That's all I remembered because I no longer felt the pain. I dozed off, and it seemed like I slept forever because, finally, my body was pain free. Deep down, I wondered would I ever wake up again. (maybe end chapter)

The bright lights and the sound of squeaky sneakers woke me up. A nurse stood over me adjusting my IV. I had never seen her before. She was a petite blond woman with big eyes and long finger nails.

"Hey there sleepy head," said the nurse. "My name is Sarah and I'll be your first shift nurse."

"It's nice to meet you Sarah," I said.

"Likewise! And I see you're a very popular person here at the hospital. People have been coming up here all day dropping off gifts. You've been sleeping for almost 24 hours. You've been in and out of sleep, though. We had to put up a *do not disturb* sign because of all the visitors and phone calls you were getting. But we did let one pretty girl come in here and sit with you while you slept. Oh she was so pretty… and there was another little boy who came, too—"

"Who was this pretty girl?" I asked excitedly and slowly, "Did she leave a name? I mean what's her name? Did she have long dark hair with pretty hazel and green eyes?" I knew the meds were affecting my speech because I was delirious. To some extent, I was confused.

"Yes, she did leave a name. I believe it was Ezra and she did have long, black hair with these green eyes," said the nurse, who was just as excited as I was. "Wait a minute," said Sarah, who reached into her long, white coat and pulled out an envelope. "The pretty girl told me to give this to you. She wanted me to give it to you as soon as you woke up. She's so sweet."

"Thank you Sarah!" I said grinning.

"You're very welcome," she said smiling. "Everything looks good, so I'll be back later to check on you."

"Okay," I said. My brown, skinny fingers ripped the envelope up so fast that I tore my fingernail. The letter was in Carolina blue and neatly hand written (crazy, LOL). The letter was from EZRA! *Awesome, she hadn't forgotten about me*, I thought to myself.

Dear Paul,

As I write this letter, I sit here and look at the wonderful man that God has put in my life. I've never met a young man so gentle, loving, caring, sincere, apologetic, sympathetic, well mannered, courageous, motivated, a man who shows chivalry and selfless. You are the epitome of what every young man should aspire to be. You have taken out the time to spend time with my brother, who is suffering from cancer. You took the time to befriend my brother when you're battling cancer yourself. Not too many people would do that, so I salute you for that. However, as I see you battle cancer, I want to remind you that you're a fighter, a fighter who didn't come this far to lose to a disease that is evil and wants to conquer your life. You're a fighter, a winner, and as the late Jim Valvano would say, "Never give up! Never give up!" You will beat cancer because I know you have the strength, will power and determination. I saw it in your eyes and I can feel it in your spirit. If God brought it to you, He'll bring you out of it. I know you'll beat cancer. Keep fighting. You're fighter. And I know a fighter when I see one. You came to win, you came to conquer, you came to kick cancer's butt. I feel in love with a fighter. And I know this fighter will win be victorious. God puts people in our lives for a reason. You came into my life and my Jericho's lives for a reason. But I'm thankful you came into my life because I've never met a young man like you before. You remind me of my father in so many ways because of your loving spirit and charismatic ways. I love you for that. Keep fighting the good fight because I know you'll be victorious. Love you dearly

Ezra

I was speechless. Tears welled up in my eyes. I gripped the letter and held it close to my heart. I smelled Ezra's perfume on the letter. I thought about the first time we had met and how lucky I was to have met her. I was beyond thrilled, and felt so many emotions: happiness, excitement, motivation, inspiration, courage, and love. I wanted to jump out of the bed and fight cancer head on. Jericho had already inspired me to fight cancer with a positive attitude, which I had begun to do, but Ezra closed the deal with her letter. It confirmed her feelings for me and vice versa. You never know how much people love you until you're on your own death bed. Cancer was a reality checker. Cancer forced people to recognize you because of its painful reality, and you recognized it as well.The constant pain, vomiting, chemo treatments, losing your hair, and damn near losing your soul were all realities of cancer. Cancer wanted to take your spirit, your soul, your will power, and your will to live. The pain was only a conduit to take your spirit. Once cancer destroyed your spirit, you died. But I wasn't going to die, not on that dark, painful day or any other day. My spirit was renewed, soul repaired, and attitude stronger than ever. Cancer was the monster and the Boogie Man, the scariest bastard of all. Cancer was going to die that day, the enemy no more. The combination of Ezra's letter and Jericho's positive attitude made me stronger and a believer, not only a survivor, but someone who would live! (maybe end chapter).

The next morning, Dr. John talked to Mom and I. Finally, I found out what was wrong with me and why I was in the hospital.

"Paul had contracted Sepsis, a blood poising that occurs when the body's immune system thrusts in to fight an infection; however, it goes strong and destroy sits very own organs and tissues. As a result, this would lead to shock of various bodily organs and death," said Dr. John.

"Oh my God! Wow! Paul could've died!" Mom said excitedly. "Thank God he's alive!"

"Sepsis is very dangerous because the immune system is weakened and it's trying to fight an infection," said Dr. John, who held my Mom's hand tightly. "More people die from sepsis each year than HIV/AIDS and any other cancer combined, according to studies. Paul is very fortunate to be alive. It's common for cancer patients to get Sepsis. However, we do everything in our power to prevent it."

"Wow! I almost died!" I said surprisingly. "So when were you all going to tell me? I mean this is my life. Right?"

"Paul," said Dr. John, placing his huge palms on my shoulders, "you were in a comatose state. The infection had already taken over your body. It's a miracle that you're still alive. Most people with a severe case of Sepsis die. You pulled through. That's awesome. A miracle. Absolutely a miracle."

There was silence. It was so quiet you could hear a mouse piss on a cotton ball in Mississippi. Everyone stood there, as if I were to explain the miracle. Heck, I was unaware of my condition. It explained why everyone paid me a visit. They must have spread the word I was dying. In that moment, I reached for both of their hands and said, "I'm thankful to be alive. God granted me another day to live and breathe this air and I want to enjoy every bit of it. I'm happy to be here. To be alive. I want to enjoy my life while I can. So I want to thank you Dr. John and your team of nurses and my Mother for her prayers. Let's move on to the next stage so I can enjoy life one breath at a time."

"You're absolutely right Paul!" said Mom, kissing my forehead. "We have to live every day to the fullest."

"That's exactly right. That's the right attitude to have," said Dr. John. "I could not have stated it better. You have the right attitude Paul. It will serve you right and take you a long way my friend during this difficult time. You're definitely a fighter."

"Thank you," I said. "I've learned to fight. That's the only way to go."

"You've made great progress and we'll going to monitor you for a few hours before we let you go home," said Dr. John.

"Awesome!" I said. "Can't wait to go home and eat some good food."

"You have to eat healthy Paul! Remember?" Mom reminded me.

"Get some rest buddy," said Dr. John

Mom kissed me on my forehead and went to the café. I took some meds before the nurses checked my vital signs and blood pressure. I fell asleep and took a long nap. I wanted to just reflect on my young life and the future. The thought that I almost died or could have died was more than an eye opener. It was another reality about the painful truth of cancer. At that moment, I was going to enjoy the cancer groups and even the chemotherapy treatments. It was time to face cancer head on like a mongoose attacking a snake.

When I awoke from my nap, there were two people sitting to my right. My vision was blurry, but when it came into focus, Malachi

Abraham, the head basketball coach at NC State University, was in my room!! Awesome, I thought to myself. Coach Abraham glided over to my bed like a ghost and extended his hand.

"Hey my buddy! Hope you're getting plenty of sleep and feeling better," said coach Abraham. "My assistant, Coach Hosea, and myself wanted to come by and check on you. We've been getting updates about your cancer from your wonderful mother. We wanted you to know that we're here for you and no need to worry about your scholarship. We will honor your scholarship, but we care more about your health at this point. Personally, I'm here because I care about you. Forget basketball, I want you to beat cancer. I want you to beat it like you beat your opponents on the basketball court. I know you will beat it. You're in my prayers, along with your awesome mother. My goal today is more about showing support to a courageous young man who is battling a deadly disease. Believe me; the Wolfpack Nation is rooting hard for you Paul!"

I was stunned, surprised and happy at the same time. Honestly, I wasn't expecting Coach Abraham to honor my scholarship, and my mind wasn't on playing basketball, ever since I had been diagnosed with cancer. Coach Abraham honoring my basketball scholarship was the icing on the cake with the cherry on top.

"Thank you so much Coach Abraham! Thank you sir. I'm so thankful and appreciative for you doing this!" I said, reaching out to hug him and Coach Hosea. Both of them hugged me lightly.

"You're very welcome Paul!" said Coach Abraham. "Please call Malachi, no need to call me coach. I'm your friend, too."

"We'll keep praying for you Paul," said Hosea. "Here is a surprise for you, too. It's from the Wolfpack basketball team."

Hosea gave me a red and white Wolfpack basketball with signatures from every player, my future teammates. Then Malachi gave me a Wolfpack notebook with messages from all of the players wishing me well and offering prayers. I knew of the players and had played against some of them in recreational basketball games. I felt like a child at Christmas opening up presents. It was beyond one the best feelings I'd ever had. I was so excited I dribbled the basketball on the floor. I showed Malachi and Hosea I still had skills when I spun the ball on continuously on my index finger.

"We can see you still got skills," said Malachi, laughing. "But we want you to get healthy, so need to impress us. We all know what you can do!"

We all laughed. We all hugged and Malachi said a small prayer, which impressed me a great deal. But before he prayed Malachi said, "I'm praying for you because I care about you. I don't care if you can't play basketball. I care about you beating this nasty disease we call cancer. Your health is way more important than shooting a basketball. Now lets' bow our heads."

Malachi kneeled down on his knees and delivered one hell of a prayer.

> *Dear Lord or heavenly Father, we come together today asking you to heal our brother from this awful disease of cancer. God we know You are more than capable than healing this fine young man. We know you can cure him and deliver him from cancer. I'm asking God that you take away this cancer and heal Paul, so that he can be healthy and strong, never allowing cancer to come into his body again. God I'm asking for you to heal Paul, give him his life back and live the life You have set for him. You're the almighty God and my prayer is that You completely eliminate the cancer in his body. Show Paul favor God and deliver this awesome and terrific young man. Amen*

"Amen!" I said, thinking about how much he cared about my health. "Thank you so much for the powerful prayer."

"You're very welcome," said Malachi, wiping tears from his eyes. Malachi hugged me and whispered in my ear, "may God give you the strength of fight! And fight hard as hell!"

Hosea hugged me too, giving me a high five and promising to stay in touch through text messages and telephone calls. Malachi and Hosea hugged Mom on the way out and reminded her she could count on them. Mom turned around with a sneaky grin on her face. I knew she was up to something. "Mom, why are you smiling," I asked, smiling. Whenever Mom smiled like that, she was up to something.

"Oh nothing Paul," she said flashing a wide grin.

"It's something, trust me!" I said laughing.

"Whatever," she said walking over and planting one her wet kisses on my forehead. She stood directly in front of me; all I could see was her neck. When she moved away, there was Ezra standing behind her holding like a hundred of *Good Well* balloons. It was great to so see her beautiful face. I felt like I was falling in love, falling very hard. Ezra wore a black leather jacket with a powdered blue shirt, faded jeans, a platinum necklace, and white Air Jordans. Her Carolina Blue nails glistened like her tiny, diamond earrings. Her hair was in a ponytail. Her green eyes pierced my heart with joy. I was nervous, just like the first time I had met her. I fumbled the sheets around my fingers. I scratched my legs constantly. My mouth was dry. I tried to speak, but nothing happened. I felt paralyzed all over again.

"Hello there handsome," said Ezra. She leaned over and planted a wet kiss on my lips. I was shocked, not because she kissed me, but how she kissed me. She kissed me as if she had found her long, lost best friend.

"I miss you so much Paul! Oh my God! You made it! I love you so much Paul! So glad you pulled through!" said Ezra. "You're a fighter!"

Ezra hugged me so hard I could barely breath. I pulled back to catch my breath. But I was happier than a hog eating corn. "I miss you too. Thanks for your love and support. Thanks for having you in my life," I said. At that moment, I wondered if I were to say I loved her, too. I felt awkward saying it, although I did love her. There was no to be shy. "I love you to Ezra. You being here mean so much to me. Something you'll never understand. Your presence here means more than love. It goes to another level."

"Paul you're very welcome!" she said through tears. "I have a surprise for you, for us! As soon as you get better, I'll tell you about the surprise."

"Oh what's wrong with telling me right now?" I asked jokingly.

"Do you really think I'm going to tell you?" Ezra said, showing her beautiful smile.

I smiled,kissed her soft lips and hugged her gently.

After several days in the hospital, it felt good to walk on my own, smell fresh air, wear nice clothes and eat good food. Being hospitalized made me more appreciative of the simple things in life. I stared at and smelled the flowers, watched the birds eat the worms from the ground, see the squirrels run up the trees and eat nuts. To hear the sound of my Air Jordan's pound the pavement felt like I had learned to walk again. The cool air touched my skin like a block of ice. It was January and cold. We had to walk a short distance to the PNC Arena. The smell of the winter breeze tickled my nostrils, and the snow covered trees and ground meant it was college basketball season. There was no better basketball state than North Carolina, forget Kentucky and Kansas. And to top it off, I was going to see the NC State Wolfpack play the hated UNC Tar Heels, two bitter rivals. I hated the Tar Heels more than anything else in the world. I only had to thank Ezra for the surprise basketball tickets. Ezra placed the tickets inside my Wolfpack jacket when I was sleeping at the hospital.

A few days later, after I had arrived home, Ezra asked me if I wanted to go out for lunch. Of course, I took her up on her offer because I wanted to get out and taste some real food, some soul food. Ezra tricked me into looking into my jacket when she said, "What was that you slid into your jacket." I said "what are you talking about?"

I was beyond clueless what she was talking about. "You know what I'm talking about!" she said. "I have no idea what you are talking about," I said laughing.

"No seriously what's in your pocket because I saw you fold a white envelope or something of that nature," said Ezra. So I reached into my left coat pocket and there was a small red and white envelope. I looked confused because I didn't know what it contained. I opened up the envelope and my eyes were the size of Carolina Beach. There were three tickets to the Wolfpack and Tar Heels basketball game. I was so happy I almost leaped across the table and hugged her.

So to be attending a Wolfpack game on a cold Saturday afternoon was beyond a blessing and excitement. Of course, I had to get the green light from Dr. John, which meant I had to be healthy. I felt good that day, no pain or anything, just a slight limp in my walk. I enjoyed looking at all of the Wolfpack fans wearing red with the Wolfpack logo. There was nothing like seeing hundreds of people wearing red flocking to the arena to see the best college basketball team in the nation. I was nervous for some reason, so I held onto Ezra's hand tightly. The adrenaline rushed through my body like waterfall. Ezra sensed my nervousness.

"Relax Paul," Ezra whispered into my ear, while massaging my hand. "Enjoy the Tar Heels whip the little wolves today!"

"Whatever," I said. "The only way you all will win is by cheating. And we know Heels are known for cheating." She sighed and shook her head.

"Losers should know when they have been conquered," she joked, laughing loudly. "I believe it's been 30 plus years since your little Wolfpack has won a national championship. Mmmm....we weren't even born yet. That was so long ago my Mom was in elementary school."

We both laughed out loud, shaking our heads in agreement. There was no comeback for that joke. I laughed because it was so funny. While we laughed, I noticed all of the people staring at us. I wondered why were they staring so hard. I wondered had they seen a tall black teenager before, which they had seen because Raleigh had thousands of Black people. Or maybe it was because I was with such a pretty girl. I noticed the smile on Ezra's face as people stared.

"Why are these people staring at us?" I asked curiously. "I know I'm walking with a pretty and hot model. You think that's it?"

"Yep! That's it baby! They see Paul with a young super model!" joked Ezra. "I really hadn't noticed them staring at us, maybe it's your nerves."

I noticed she kept smiling. "Oh yeah, that's it, you're right. They see the teenager with cancer with a super model. And they're wondering how in the hell did I get this pretty super model," I joked.

"You never know," said Ezra, who had a wicked grin on her face. She knew something but remained calm and kept smiling.

We approached gate #1 and a tall white man with a goatee smiled as he took our tickets. "This way young man and young woman. Follow the hostess," he said in his thick North Carolinian accent. "Thank you sir," said the both of us.

"Enjoy the game and go Wolfpack!" he said.

"Go Wolfpack!" I said.

"Go Heels!" said Ezra.

I rolled my eyes at Ezra and laughed. We followed the hostess to an express elevator that would take us to the luxury suites. The hostess looked like a young teenager, which she probably was, a student at that. She led us to a large elevator decorated in Wolfpack red with pictures of famous Wolfpack players. They had framed pics of the Wolfpack 1974 & 1983 National Championship teams. There were pictures of legendary basketball players like David Thompson, Monte Towe, Tommy Burleson, Dereck Whittenburg, Sidney Lowe, Thurl Bailey, and the late, great Jimmy Valvano. Jimmy V was his nickname. All of these basketball players were before my time. It was exciting to look at the great basketball history of the NC State Wolfpack. It was great to go back down memory lane. Then I returned my attention back to Ezra and the hostess.

"We aren't sitting in the regular seats?" I said to no one in particular. "So why are we going to the luxury suites?" I asked the hostess, who was petite and dressed in a red and white Wolfpack skirt. She turned around and flashed a smile.

"I don't know. I guess you're a popular guy!" she said, giggling as she led us into the luxury suite.

"Yeah right," I said, laughing.

"You'll see," said the hostess, still smiling from ear to ear.

I turned and glanced at Ezra, who had a smirk on her face. Ezra looked like she had swallowed a goat. She was beyond guilty.

"What?" Ezra said sarcastically, smiling at me the whole time. She remained quiet, but kept grinning.

I shook my head and smiled. The elevator took us straight to the suite, which was spacious with red and white plush carpet. The leather sofas were black and red with white, cushy pillows. The walls were neatly decorated with all types of basketball memorabilia on the walls. There were several people there wearing either suits and ties or Wolfpack sweatshirts. Food was everywhere, pizza, hot dogs, hamburgers, chicken, steaks, crab legs, and fish. Popcorn and soda machines lined the back of the walls. There was a huge window in the center of the suite that gave everyone a bird's eye view of the basketball court. The clear window reminded me of a humongous aquarium without the water. The players weren't on the court yet, just the cheerleaders and dance girls. But I was still curious to why we were in the suite, and not sitting in the crowd. It was just a thought.

"Hey there! You must be Paul!" said a tall bald headed man wearing a Wolfpack jacket.   "My name is Judge Peters. We've been waiting to meet you."

Judge Peters extended his hand. His grip was firm. My big hand slid into his gigantic hand like a glove, one big hand to another. "My name is Paul Christian, sir, I mean Mr. Peters. It's nice to meet you," I said.

"Please call me Judge," he said. "I don't like to feel old." He laughed, sounded like a cartoon character.

"And this must be Ezra," said Judge.

"Yes, hello Judge," said Ezra. "It's nice to put a name with a face. Thank you for this opportunity."

"You're very welcome. But I want to thank you for telling us about Paul, for allowing us to meet Paul. We appreciate people like Paul who is fighting the fight, the courageous fight, the real fight! They're the ones who fight and never complain," said Judge.

"You're welcome!" said Ezra, smiling so hard you could see both of her dimples. She winked at me and kept smiling.

"Thank you Judge," I said. "I appreciate the opportunity to be here."

"You are most welcome!" said Judge, patting me on my shoulder. Then I turned my attention to Ezra, wondering what did she do. She flashed that gorgeous smile of her.

"I called the Valvano Club on your behalf. They like to support kids and teenagers who are fighting cancer. They like to make their dreams and wishes come true. Since you're a die-hard NC State Wolfpack fan, I had to call them and tell them how you love the Pack and the good things you're doing in the community," said Ezra, who was squeezing my hand tightly. Ezra thought I needed her approval. I was excited to the 10th degree. She thought enough of me to reach out to the Valvano Club meant so much. It brought back memories of me and Dad attending the Wolfpack games.

"Baby I'm in heaven!" I laughed. "I get to see my Wolfpack play the stinking Tar Heels. This is a dream come true." We embraced each other and I planted a kiss on her cheek. I stroked her long, black hair and kissed her forehead. I stared into her eyes long enough to see my own reflection. I saw the beauty of her soul, her spirit, and her selflessness. I found a goldmine. I whispered in her "you're the best! Thanks again!"

"I want you all to enjoy yourself today. Eat all of the food you want. Drink all of the Pepsi, Mountain Dew you want. We have a lot of healthy food for you, too, Paul. Take as much as you want. Just enjoy yourself!" said Judge. "You can either watch the game up here in the suite or you all can watch the game behind the Wolfpack bench. This is your day Paul, enjoy it with Ezra."

"Thank you so much!" We both said.

"Well I have to be careful what I eat, but I'm definitely eating," I said. "That's a fact baby girl."

"Alright then! Let's get our grub on!" said Ezra, using an old slang word for eating a lot of food. "I'm going to start on this pepperoni pizza."

"Awesome!" I said, as I grabbed two pieces of baked fish, celery and carrots. I figured I'd try to eat healthy, although the fried chicken was calling my name. The plan was for us to eat as much as possible without puking and go watch the game behind the Wolfpack bench. We figured it was best to be surrounded kids our age and to see my future teammates. I ate only three pieces of fish and some carrots. My appetite disappeared, but Ezra ate everything from pizza to fish to chicken and meatballs.I envied her because she could eat whatever she wanted. How could a pretty girl eat so much and keep a nice shape, I thought to myself.

Instead of taking the elevator, we decided to walk down the long stairs, besides I needed the exercise. I held Ezra's hand and walked slowly. The steps were small and steep, making me walk on my tip toes to avoid an embarrassing fall. My legs felt heavy like sandbags. Ezra held my arm to give her balance, but it felt like she was pulling on it. I was fine with it as long as we didn't tumble down the steps and be on social media. So I wrapped my arm around Ezra so that she could lean on me.

Wolfpack fans were screaming so loud I could barely hear Ezra talking to me. I leaned down so that I could hear her lovely voice.

"This is so exciting! Wow! They are really turned up!" said Ezra, who seemed more excited than me. "We're going to have so much fun."

"Yeah it's so loud my eardrum is about to bust," I yelled into Ezra's ear. "But this is how we do it in Wolfpack Nation baby. We bring the pain! I love it! If my eardrum bust and we whip the Tar Heels butt, it'll be worth it."

"It's going to take more than this loud noise to beat my Heels baby!" screamed Ezra, which almost burst my eardrums.

"You're in denial," I said. "Never underestimate the power of denial. But you'll be okay, though."

We both laughed, although we couldn't hear each other's laughter because of the noise. I pulled her closer to my body because the fans were so happy; they were jumping out into the aisles. Some of the fans wore Wolfpack masks with sharp teeth. I swear they looked like real wolves, especially with red eyes that glowed in the dark. Yes, the light crew was dimming the lights off and on to give the arena a wildlife effect. With all of the Wolfpack fans screaming, yelling, and howling like wolves, it felt like we were lost in the wilderness. It seemed like the closer we got to our seats, the rowdier the fans were.

"If I weren't sick, I'd jump up and down too," I joked. "I'd be jumping and hollering like a wolf, jumping all over people."

"I know you would! You're crazy just like these pitiful Wolfpack fans! Y'all have no home training," said Ezra, who was now fully hugging me. "Piss poor upbringing."

I laughed. Then noticed there was a man with a flashlight motioning us to go in a certain direction. He was telling us this was our seat. At that moment, I noticed the noise got much louder. The students started yelling, "There he goes! There he goes! There he goes!"

Honestly, I had no idea who they were chanting about or why they were chanting. I looked at Ezra and gave her a confused facial expression. I eased Ezra in front of me and guided her to her seat because the isle was smaller than a shoebox. Ezra smelled sweet like honey. I wanted to just smell her. When I sat down, the crowd started chanting again, "there he goes! There he goes! That's our man! Right there!" Then a bright light shone directly over us for a brief second. *Wait a minute, are they talking about me? I thought to myself. Fighting cancer made me forget about to some degree I was a really good basketball player.*

"You think they're talking about me Ezra?" I asked. She smiled weirdly, as if she knew something.

"Umm...I...I...don't know," stuttered Ezra. "Maybe they are...I...mean...who…knows!"

Ezra giggled, smirking the whole time. Ezra knew something. Then I heard a familiar voice shout out, "hey there Paul!" It turned around and it was Coach Malachi, grinning like a kid in a candy store.

"Paul this is your special day. We're going to honor you as a future Wolfpack player and an honorary captain," said Malachi. "There's another guy that's going to be an honorary captain, too. He's a future Wolfpacker, too."

"Wow! Are you serious?" I asked, still surprised and shocked. "This can't be real! No way!"

I was stunned beyond belief. I was so stunned I couldn't talk, sweat poured down my face like rain.

"It's for real Paul. This is no joke. This is the real deal," said Malachi. "You deserve it."

"They're honoring you today bae!" said Ezra, who leaned in and kissed me on my lips.

"So you've known about this for how long?" I asked, kissing and hugging her at the same time. "This is nice."

"We'll be honoring you at halftime," said Malachi, patting me on my shoulder as he walked towards the bench.

"Thanks again," I said as I turned to Ezra and gave her another kiss on her cheek.

"You're certainly welcomed Paul!" she said.

I leaned back in my chair and waited for the game to start. I pulled Ezra close to my chest. She laid her head on my chest and held my hand. It seemed like confirmation that we were a couple. We sat quietly as the players trotted out onto the court. A bright light shadowed the players as they warmed up. I imagined myself out there playing, shooting jump shots and lay ups. I pictured Dad and Mom in the audience cheering me on, along with Ezra and Jericho. I was going to play for the Wolfpack. There was a time when I thought I was going to die, because I had no hope, only a negative attitude. But that seemed so long ago. So I twirled my fingers in Ezra's hair and dragged my forefinger down the middle of her back, thinking about how I could repay her back for this experience. The more I caressed her back, the more relax she became. She had temporarily dozed off. I kissed her forehead and continued to caress her back.

Suddenly, the crowd booed loudly as the stinky Tar Heels ran out onto the court. The booing was so loud that Ezra body jerked.

"Are   you   okay?"   I   asked   her.

"Yeah! I'm fine," said Ezra, who was still dazed from all of the noise. "Wow! The game is about to start."

"Yep! The Wolfpack is about to tear those cheaters up! Well, unless those cheaters cheat!" I said laughing.

"Dream on loser!" said Ezra, laughing so softly.

"We'll see. Get your Kleenex ready!" I said.

After each team shot around, the players went to their benches and waited for their introduction. The Tar Heels were announced first, and I heard the loudest boos ever! The crowd booed so loud, I could feel my ear drums slowly tear. The noise was so loud that the Tar Heels starting lineup just ran out onto the court because they couldn't even hear their names being called.

When it came time to introduce the Wolfpack starting lineup, I got goose bumps because I pictured myself experiencing the exact same thing one day. The public announcers flashed a bright light over the team and called out their names while the rap song, *We Started From The Bottom* by Drake played in the background. When the first player name was announced, the crowd went into a loud frenzy, so loud you could barely hear the player's name.

I already knew most of the players' name, so it wasn't a problem for me. Ezra covered her ears because the noise was too loud. The Wolfpack fans were the best and the craziest. Fans were jumping up and down and all over each other. With the darkness, the fireworks, and the sounds of wolves howling, the PNC arena resembled a jungle on the 4th of July! Then the crowd really went wild when they called out a kid named *David Thompson*. All of the fans chanted, "DT! DT! DT!"

DT was a high-flying, athletic All American basketball shooting guard for the Wolfpack. He was the best player in the country bar none.

He was the primary reason the Wolfpack had a winning record. DT was about 6′6, toned like an action figure, had great dribbling skills, could shoot the ball well and could jump out of the gym like a kangaroo on steroids. He was the primary reason I wanted to join the Wolfpack. DT was like Michael Jordan, could slam dunk anyway possible.

"Take a good look at him!" I shouted to Ezra. "He's going to score about 50 points tonight on your dirty Tar Heels because nobody can stop DT except God Himself!"

"Okay! We'll see!" shouted back Ezra, who was waving her hand in my face very wildly. "Let's see if you're talking after taking this "L" tonight."

"Someone needs their meds right now because they're talking delusional, non-sense!" joked Ezra, who was laughing so hard she almost choked on her soda. "Besides, we have a better coach young man! Watch this blowout baby!"

"Okay!" I said grinning. Both teams went to the middle of the court for the jump ball. The referee through the ball up high in the air and a Wolfpack player tipped it to DT. DT dribbled, crossed-over a Tar Heels player and hit a long 3-pointer. The crowd went wild. Then DT stole the inbound pass for an easy two-handed dunk. The Tar Heels inbounded the ball and lost it to a Wolfpack player. The point guard passed it to DT, who drained another 3-pointer. The crowd really lost their minds because the Wolfpack had an 8 point lead. The Tar Heels called a quick time out.

"Yeah baby! Yeah baby! Look at the Pack! Look at them!" I screamed to no one in particular! I was so excited that I almost fell down and my Jordan's came off.

"It's not over yet. They're just lucky Paul! We'll be back!" said Ezra, who was shocked. She kept shaking her head as if something was in there.

"I know you're surprised baby girl!" I said. "Y'all won't cheat yourself out of this butt whipping we're going to deliver on cheating Heels today."

"Whatever! We have time to make a comeback!" said Ezra, who was holding her ears because the crowd was so loud.

After the timeout, the Tar Heels missed a 3-pointer that led to a long rebound and a Wolfpack fast break. Of course, DT was the recipient of a monstrous slam dunk. The Tar Heels players started to panic and committed turnover after turnover. And the Wolfpack made them pay to the fullest extent. The Wolfpack converted five turnovers into 15 points. Before the Tar Heels scored their first basket, the score was 25-2 in the Wolfpack's favor. The noise level crept to new levels, as fans were covering up their ears. I pulled Ezra close to me and covered up her ears. Plus, I wanted to hold her.

"Yay-hoo! Go Pack!" I screamed out.

"That'll be you next year out there, killing the Tar Heels!" yelled out an older man sitting behind me.

"Yes sir! It will be!" I yelled, so happy to see my team winning. "It'll definitely happen. Yes, God willing, it'll happen."

I turned my attention back to the action on the basketball court. The Wolfpack were scoring baskets at will. The Tar Heels players were making so many mistakes, that the game resembled a *Little Rascals* episode. Slam dunk after slam dunk, basket after basket, DT and the Wolfpack were killing the Tar Heels. I yelled so hard, my throat started itch. The arena sounded like a pack of wolves hunting for their prey. ThreeWolfpack fans were so excited they ran out onto the court to celebrate. All three of them had on no shirts and shoes. One of them was a fat kid who looked like Humpty Dumpty as he ran onto the court. Security guards chased them down and escorted them out of the arena, not before they screamed, "WolfpackFor Life!" Then the crowd howled like wolves and chanted, "WolfpackFor Life! WolfpackFor Life! WolfpackFor Life!"

The score was 60-20 with 3:16 left before halftime. The Wolfpack had a commanding lead and a blowout was in the making. Ezra was too embarrassed to watch the game. Her head was buried underneath her coat.

"This is awful! I want to just puke! I can't take this killing. They're slaughtering us like animals!" said Ezra, who tried to hide her laughter but couldn't. "This is incredible. They suck right now. My goodness! God help them!"

I smirked. And twirled my fingers in her hair."Poor baby! Are you okay? Do you want a pacifier?" I joked. "Because I have one in my pocket."

Ezra rolled her eyes and pinched me. I pretended it hurt, and made a baby sound. At that moment, two Security guards in a thick, leather jackets approached us and told us to follow them. Ezra tapped me on my shoulder and smiled and whispered, "It's your time to shine!"Then she kissed me on my forehead.

"Follow us," said the tall security guard.

"Okay," we both said at the same time. I held Ezra's hand and held it close to my heart. Then I caressed the back of her neck with my left hand. She felt my heart pounding and the wetness of my shirt because she wiped the sweat from underneath my shirt. I leaned over and said, "Thank you again. Thank you a thousand times baby girl! I'll never forget this moment."

We followed them to the other side of the court to a dark, long walkway, the same walkway the Wolfpack players run through for every game. For a moment, I prepared myself to run out of the tunnel. As the time winded down on the game clock, one of Coach Malachi's assistant coaches came over and explained to me the details, along with a tall, clean cut White man, who looked like he should be in an All State insurance commercial. Malachi's assistant coach was a short, stocky guy, with big hands that reminded you of a catcher's mitten. His name was Habakkuk, a really cool dude.

"What's going on my man Paul," said Habakkuk, who gripped my hand so hard, it turned red.

"Just enjoying this butt whipping my Wolfpack is putting on the Tar Heels," I said laughing.

"That's the attitude right there man! Can't wait to see you here next year!" said Habakkuk, showing all of his teeth."Here are what you all going to do. Follow this gentleman, Peter Jones, to the middle of the court and they're going to honor you and another young man for your community service.

"Really!Community service? Are you for real? I thought I was being honored as a future Wolfpacker and an honorary captain?" I asked curiously. My nerves shook me to the core and my palms were sweaty. "So I'm being honored for something else?"

"Not exactly Paul. You will still be honored as a future Wolfpacker and as an honorary captain. That still stands. However, you're also being honored today for a good cause," said Peter Jones, who was so happy and excited that he was jumping up and down.

"Wait…wait…wait…what am I being honored for again?" I asked again, because I was beyond shocked and now nervous. I wondered what had I actually done to deserve an award. Me being excited was an understatement.

"You'll well deserving of it," said Ezra, who had a smile on her face like the Joker.

"So what else do you know?" I asked jokingly. "What's next, Jericho parachuting through the roof on a donkey?"

Ezra and Peter Jones laughed loudly, giving each other a high-five.

"This part is a surprise but I'm sure you'll appreciate it," said Peter Jones. "You're a good kid."

"Alrighty!I said, nervous as a kid learning how to ride a bike for the first time. I wondered who was the other person being honored, and what community service had I been doing. I was about to find out soon because the horn sounded and it was halftime.

As we followed Peter Jones to the center of the basketball court, I noticed a small and skinny kid standing there with two women. Their backs were to me so I couldn't see their faces. When I walked onto the court holding Ezra's hand, the crowd erupted, shouting "P.C.! P.C! P.C.!"

"Wow! This is exciting!" I shouted to Ezra. "I can't believe they're talking about me!"

"This is very unbelievable," said Ezra, who leaned in to me and wrapped her arm around my waist. "You're definitely a crowd favorite.

At the middle of the court stood the Wolfpack cheerleaders, who had created a huge circle with an opening at two openings. The Packettes, a bunch of pretty petite girls who danced and cheered, raised their pompoms high in the air, as if they were saluting us. And the closer we got I recognized my mother standing in the middle of the court with a bouquet of flowers. Mom wore a red and white Wolfpack sweater and some blue jeans with white Air Jordan's. Her pretty smile resembled that of a young college student. Heck, Mom was pretty enough to be a cheerleader, definitely athletic enough with those long legs.

"Hey Mom! Give me a kiss!" I said hugging her so hard. "You knew about this, too?" I asked, still hugging her tightly.

"Of course not Paul!" said Mom, giggling like a little girl. "We've known about this for a long time. Just had to keep it up under wraps."

"Y'all did a great job in keeping it a secret," I said, trying not to get emotional and not cry. "But who is this other person they're honoring-"

"Who's that boy with the big, canoe feet?" said a loud and familiar voice. "I hope you didn't kick anyone with those craw feet of yours."

I turned around and it was my buddy Jericho, strutting up the court, arm and arm, with onebeautiful Wolfpack cheerleader and his lovely mother, Mrs. Walls. Jericho walked with a slight limp, as if he were trying to be cool. Dressed in an oversize red and white Wolfpack Jersey with a white Nike cap, Jericho appeared to be wearing his father's shirt. He looked smaller, too, very small. We ran up to each other and embraced each other tightly, dapping each other up with high-fives.

"What's up my brother?" I screamed out. "Man it's so good to see you! It's been a long time!"

"Yes it has been a long time! I'm so glad you made it! So happy to see you alive! God I love you man!" said Jericho, hugging me so tightly. "It wasn't your time to die because God don't have any shoes to fit those large, dinosaur feet of yours!"

I laughed so hard I got the hiccups. No matter the situation or environment, Jericho made me laugh. His happy spirit was contagious. You wanted to be happy like him, no Debbie downer.

"How long did you know about them honoring us? Because I know you knew?" I asked Jericho, who pretended not to hear me. "I'll wait!"

"I have no clue to what you're talking about!" said Jericho, laughing so hard he was shaking.

"Oh you knew! You little rascal!" I said, playfully jabbing him in the ribs. At that moment, Peter Jones told us to turn our attention to the crowd because they were about to honor the both of us.

"In a few minutes I'm going to explain why you two are here and present you both an award. So when I started addressing the crowd, you two stay about five feet behind me," said Peter Jones, who was very animated in his explanation. He reminded me of a conductor in an orchestra. All he needed was a baton. Peter smiled like the Joker. It was hard not to laugh. When Peter wasn't looking, Jericho put his fingers in his mouth and stretched his cheeks, mocking the smile of Peter. It was hilarious, made my stomach hurt.

"Okay! That'll work," I said to Peter.

"Yep! Sure will!" said Jericho, who was trying not to laugh. Mom saw me laughing and shook her head, knowing I was laughing about something.

Peter Jones walked slowly to the middle of the court as if he were the King, smiling ear-to-ear. Although Jericho and I laughed at him, we really liked him. My thoughts were to have as much fun as possible after almost dying. Cancer taught me to enjoy every precious moment of life, laughter helped.

"Can I get everyone's attention please? Today we would like to honor two extraordinary teenagers for their commitment and excellence in the community," said Peter, who was smiling really hard. "Paul Christian and Jericho Walls are both volunteers at the Wildlife Bird Sanctuary, a place where they rehabilitate injured birds. Paul and Jericho are both group leaders to other cancer-stricken children who are participants at the Bird Sanctuary. These outstanding individuals have nursed back several birds to health and released them back into the wild. In addition, Paul volunteers his time at the UNC Children's Hospital, reading to them and encouraging them to fight and never give up their fight with cancer. Their commitments are valued and illustrate a selfless and courageous act on their part. Furthermore, and what is so unique about this situation is that Paul is battling cancer, and Jericho's cancer is in remission. Because of their caring attitude and awesomeness, we at North Carolina State University would like to honor these outstanding individuals today. Paul Christian and Jericho Walls are the recipients of the "Jimmy V Never Give Up Award". This award goes to the people who exemplify the values, hard work, selfless act, generosity, and fighting spirit of Jim Valvano. Paul and Jericho are well deserving of this prestigious award. Also, and because of his fight with cancer, great work in the community, and exceptional grades, Paul Christian has earned the "Courage of Heart Academic

Scholarship" to attend North Carolina State University for four years to study Zoology. So everyone, please stand up and give these two young men a round of applause."

I was so shocked and excited I couldn't move. When Peter Jones handed me the award, my hands quivered violently, palms were sweaty and leg cramps paralyzed my movement. I felt like they were in concrete, jerking them quickly so that I didn't stand like a statue. The thunderous clapping and cheering from the crowd made me feel beyond special and important. I cleared my throat and took a deep breath before I spoke to the crowd.

"Thank you! I want to give a big thank you to the greatest university in the country, North Carolina State University, the home of the Wolfpack! WolfpackNation!" I screamed in the microphone. "I want you all to know I'm more than happy to be the recipient of the *Jimmy V Never Give Up Award* and *Courage of Heart Academic Scholarship*. This is a dream come true. I'll give this university all of my sweat and tears and then some. I'll represent this university to the fullest extent with hard work, courage, and illustrating the characteristics of the great Jimmy V. This has been a long journey, but to make it this far, to change my attitude towards a deadly disease, I owe it to my good friend Jericho Walls, who helped change my attitude into something positive. Jericho isn't aware of his positive impact on my life. But if it weren't for Jericho, I wouldn't be here to accept this prestigious award. I would've given up a long time ago. I would have died at the hospital. But the strength, the courage, the struggle, I got from you Jericho, I love you man! You believed in me and made me fight. I saw your positive attitude and how you dealt with cancer, and it changed me for the better. I'm fighting the fight, and never giving up like Jimmy V did. You're the brother I never had. I love you my brother. You're the best friend ever! What I've learned more than anything else about cancer is that you can't let cancer define you. You don't let cancer control you, beat you, destroy you, or even kill you. You define yourself by how you live through cancer, still accomplishing your goals, and by living your life. If I were writing a book about my life, cancer would be a footnote, a sidebar, just a simple hurdle, nothing more, and nothing else. Getting diagnosed with cancer can shake up your world when you're a 17 year-old teenager who loves basketball. At first, I let cancer eat me away, destroy me as a person and tear my spirit into pieces, my will to live. I hated everyone, everything, and life itself. How in the hell does cancer pick and choose me? A healthy and athletic teenager! God you know this isn't fair. No way! My Dad died of cancer! So now I was going to die, too. Poor Mom! She lost her husband to cancer, and now she was going to lose her only son, too! That's what I thought at the time.Whenever you have cancer, you, and you only you, dictate how you live your life, why you live your life and to continue to exist because it's your life. Not cancer. Cancer doesn't get its way. You control cancer. Cancer doesn't control you. I learned that from you Jericho Walls! God put you in my life for this very reason, to battle this deadly disease and to conquer it. God Bless you Jericho! Love you my brother! I love you so much buddy!"

I lifted Jericho up and hugged him so hard barely breath. The tears rolled down my face like a waterfall, no longer able to hold them back. Tears soaked my sweatshirt. I could feel the wetness sticking to my chest. All of the pains, pent up frustration, disappointment in not playing high school basketball, Dad's death, almost dying, were now tears of joy. The tears emptied out of my body like a river pours into an ocean. I had been liberated. The pain and misery were washed away forever. My dreams returned. I had won! No longer was I suffering. I was free, free like the sparrow with the broken wings, ready to fly away.

"We did it buddy! We did it!" I whispered into Jericho's ear.

"No you did it Paul! This is all you my brother! This is all you, believing in yourself and wanting to beat cancer!" said Jericho, wiping a tear from his eyes.

Then Peter Jones handed the microphone to Jericho, who was still wiping away tears but smiling.

"I just want to say first and foremost that I love you, too, Paul Christian. You're definitely the big brother I never had. Just remember that God puts people in our lives for a reason, and He put us together because He knew we needed each other. We could benefit from each other. And we have done exactly that. But the praise and hard work goes to you my brother. You won! Because, you kept fighting and never gave up. You never gave up my brother. I love you more Paul Christian. I love you more!"

The crowd erupted into a loud roar. All I heard was clapping and hollering, people screaming, "Way to go! You're the man!" Everyone was crying, there wasn't a dry eye anywhere. Mom and Mrs. Walls were crying hysterically. Ezra was now in my arms, face in my chest, crying. I wiped the tears away and gently kissed her forehead.

"Great speech Paul! I'm so proud of you! I love so much! You're unquestionably a role model for children with cancer. And I absolutely love that characteristic about you!" said Ezra.

"Thank you so much Ezra!" I said, hugging her tighter. "I love you too, Ezra Walls, I love you so much. You're one of the best things to ever happen to me. It's funny, if it weren't for me having cancer, we'd never met. You can always find something positive in a negative situation. I found a great friend and brother in Jericho, and I found a fantastic and beautiful girlfriend in you!"

"I know I'm the lucky one Paul! I'm the one blessed to have met a young man that's a fighter and beyond special!" said Ezra, who wiped a tear from her. "I learned more from you in a few months than I have in my whole life. That's awesome! Thank you for having me in your life!"

"You're very welcome my love! Likewise, I'm thankful God put you in my life," I said, continuing to hug her tightly. By now, Mom and Mrs. Walls were hugging us, including Jericho. We were now standing in a circle, hugging each other and wiping the tears from our eyes. It was truly a precious moment, something I'd never forget.

"You two boys are definitely are an inspiration to the thousands of children suffering from cancer. The hope you all give the children will encourage them and inspire them to fight the good fight against cancer and to never give up!" said Mom. "Both of your fathers are looking down at the two of you and smiling! Job well done fellas is what they're saying."

"Paul and Jericho, I couldn't be prouder of two men who have embraced a deadly disease and determined to fight if off," said Mrs. Walls. "I know Jericho's cancer is in remission, but for him to inspire you Paul speaks volumes. This is wonderful!"

"Yes it is!" I said, as I started to walk slowly, hand in hand with Ezra.

The crowd continued to cheer our names as we all walked off the court. Peter Jones followed behind us and motivated the crowd to make more noise. For that day, in that moment, I felt like I didn't have cancer, no side effects, no nothing, just a wonderful feeling of being a regular teenager. It was the most exciting day in my life, not to mention the Wolfpack beat the Tar Heels on that chilly Saturday afternoon, allowing me to feel like a winner all around. That day was the beginning of the new me!

"That happened 20 years ago, almost 21 years ago, to be exact. I learned so much about myself and how to deal with challenges in life. As bad as it was to have cancer, it forced me to make a decision: either deal with it or let it kill you. Jericho helped me with that," I explained, "And that's the same approach I use when I rehabilitate birds of any kind, especially sparrows, my favorite bird. These birds have broken wings or are sick. But in order for them to get back to health, they need help someone to nurture them and make them healthy again. That is the job I love so much. I'm that positive reinforcement that allows them to live again and to fly again.The same way Jericho did for me so many years ago," I said to little Jerry, my 10 year-old son.

"So that's the main reason why I love nursing birds back to health, and that's the story of how I became so fascinated with birds," I said to little Jerry.

"Awesome Dad. You're doing something great to save birds!" said little Jerry. "And Dad is that the reason why I'm named after uncle Jericho?"

"Exactly! The primary reason you're named after me," said Jericho, patting little Jerry on the head. "See I had to help your Dad out because he was lost like stray dog, and since I helped him out, he had to name you after me! Plus, I'm a better basketball player than him!"

The three of us busted out laughing, shaking my head at the hilarious Jericho. He was still the same funny guy after all of these years, just older and bald like me, and now his brother-in-law.

"Jericho you should've been a comedian," I said laughing.

"Yep! Should have been a comic instead of the head basketball coach at North Carolina State University," said Ezra. "He's beyond funny."

"It's amazing how we both loved birds and basketball. I was the high school and college All American who played for the Wolfpack, won a national title and made it to the NBA. But I became an ornithologist and zoologist. And Jericho becomes the head coach of the Wolfpack," I laughed, very proud of my brother-in-law.

"It makes sense because we're both doing something we love," said Jericho, giving me a high-five. "That's the way it's supposed to be."

"Alright everybody, the moment is here. The sun is shining, let's do it," I said. "I will grab the bird cage. Someone go get both of the grandmothers, Grandma Christian and Grandma Walls."

As I grabbed bird cage, I leaned over and kissed Ezra, my beautiful wife, something I do whenever we have this special occasion. The kiss symbolized me being cancer-free for 20 years, and it meant something else would be free that day, too.

Jericho and I led the way up the small hill in my massive backyard. The sun was shining on our heads, sweat dripping everywhere. But whenever we have this occasion, we're too excited to feel the heat. Once at the top of the hill, we placed the bird cage on the five-foot high wooden platform, with a long, thick, wide beam made for walking. Simultaneously, Jericho and I opened up the door of the bird cage. The sparrow walked out. And it flew away. Flying high into the sky and disappearing into the clouds.

"He's free now," whispered Jericho.

"Yes he is!" I said, smiling.

And finally, after 20 years, we were free, too, free from cancer. But in the beginning, Jericho was free from cancer, and I learned how to free myself from the fear of cancer. As I continued to look into the sky, I remembered my time struggling with cancer and the long journey to recovery. All I could think of was Dad smiling, telling me to, "Never give up! Never give up!"

And I didn't.

The End

www.ingramcontent.com/pod-product-compliance
Lightning Source LLC
Chambersburg PA
CBHW040832010826
48978CB00012BB/726